CYNTHIA HICKEY

SAY BYE TO MOMMY
A Highland Springs suspense novel, book 2
By Cynthia Hickey

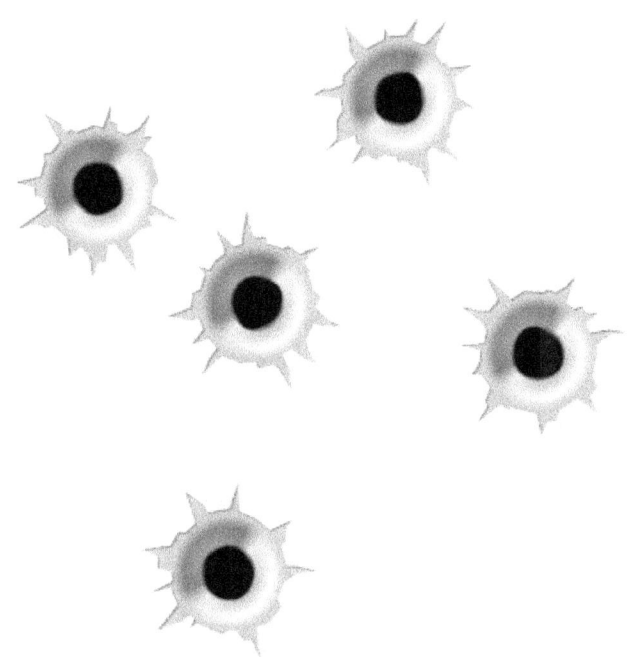

Published b Winged Publications

ISBN-13: 978-1-0881-3893-9

CHAPTER ONE

Ah. She spotted the perfect target. A little girl in a blue dress, the ruffles along the hem torn. Her socks sagging. Dirt marred the chubby legs. Mama browsed the women's clothes, leaving the little one standing in the back of the shopping cart.

The Child Saver as she liked to call herself, quietly stepped up to the cart and pushed it around the corner.

"Say bye to Mommy."

She grinned and continued to the door. It didn't take long for the mother to start shouting her daughter's name.

"So, you're Lacey. I think we should call you Lauren to avoid confusion, don't you?" She made her way halfway through the parking lot before the store alert sounded.

The Child Saver quickly stashed the little girl in the back of her van and drove away. When the little girl started crying, The Child Saver turned up the radio. Classical music always tamed them. Not as well as a leather strap, but that was at home.

Thirty minutes later, she turned "Lauren" over to

Betty to clean up and post her picture on the website, then The Child Saver headed to her job. Not the one making her money, but the one that made her respectable.

She laughed. Right under the good sheriff's nose and no one suspected a thing. The field was ripe for harvest in the mountains. Plenty of poor children in need of a better home. She'd take what she could, then move on.

Sharlene Camenetti watched the local news, her sheriff badge showing signs of wear and tear after a hard-fought second election. She sagged against the edge of her desk. It had been a hard year, emotionally. After Lars Townsend, her half-brother, aka The Silencer, she'd lived day-to-day with more questions than purpose. Thankfully, not much happened in Highland Springs other than graffiti and domestic disputes.

Everis Hayes, an agent with the Arkansas Bureau of Investigations, had gone dark almost as soon as he'd left her. She shouldn't be surprised. There had been no promises made between the two of them. Still, the ache in her heart refused to go away and it had nothing to do with too much coffee.

"Hey, boss, we got a hysterical mom outside." Deputy Mark Mayfield stuck his head in her office.

"Send her in."

"She refuses. Says she needs to stay out in the open."

Shar frowned, then shrugged. She'd heard weirder things. Clicking off the television, she followed Mayfield.

A young woman dressed in faded leggings and an oversized tee shirt stood under a tree, her eyes darting up and down the street. As Shar and Mayfield approached, she whirled. "You have to help me." Mascara tracks ran down her cheeks. "Someone stole my baby."

Shar glanced at Mayfield. "Come inside and tell us everything."

"No. What if she's looking for me? Lacey is smart. She's only five, but she'll know to come here." She covered her face with her hands and collapsed.

Mayfield rushed forward to catch her before she fell and lowered her to the sidewalk. "Sheriff?"

"We'll do the interview out here." Shar sat next to the woman. "What's your name?"

"Lynn Tales. We were shopping at Lucky's, and I was checking the price on a tee shirt, just for a second, when I turned around and the cart was gone. I yelled Lacey's name, then ran for the customer service desk. They locked down the store, but it was too late. She wasn't there."

"Could she have wandered off?"

"No. I heard someone, a woman, tell her to say bye to Mommy. I thought they were talking about someone else." Her sobs increased.

"Do you have a photo of your daughter?" Shar peeled the woman's hands from her face and peered into her eyes. "I need you to focus, Ms. Tales. I'll do everything in my power to find your daughter, but I need your help." There were few things worse than a missing child. Shar couldn't imagine the woman's pain.

"I have a few in my backpack." She pulled an army-green pack toward her. She dug out a picture of a pretty little blue-eyed, blond child in a My Little Pony sweatshirt.

"What was she wearing when she disappeared?" Shar took the photo and handed it to Mayfield.

"A blue ruffled dress." The woman clutched Shar's hands. "Please get her back."

"I'll do everything in my power. What's your address?"

The woman paled. "I'm, uh, in between places right now."

"You're homeless?"

She nodded and ducked her head. "We've been living under the overpass for two weeks after my boyfriend kicked us out."

"We'll need his name and address." Hopefully, they'd find the little girl scared, but safe, with the ex.

"Roger Holden." She rattled off the address of an apartment complex. "She isn't there, though. I already checked."

"We'll still question him." Shar stood and helped the woman to her feet. "Deputy Mayfield will bring you a doughnut and a cup of coffee. Can we get you anything else?"

"I can stay here?" Hope flickered in her eyes.

"For now." Shar patted her on the shoulder and hurried to her jeep. While she walked, she radioed Pinson. "You're with me. Come on."

"Now?"

"Yes, now." Shar opened the driver's door as Pinson jogged out the door of the building and to the passenger side. She threw Pinson a weak smile, and gestured toward Mayfield. "Sound the Amber alert." She sped from the parking lot.

Pinson had lightened up a bit since being assigned to her office, but Shar didn't need anyone to tell her he still resented working for a woman, despite having gone on a few dates with her sister, Candy.

"Where are we going?" He asked, clicking his seatbelt into place.

"To question a man about a missing child."

Pinson jerked his head. "Isolated incident?"

She cut him a sideways glance. "Yes, why?"

"Missouri has had a rash of children under five go missing." He shrugged. "It could be related."

"It could." But Shar wasn't about to create a panic by linking Lacey's disappearance with those children. Not unless she had absolute proof.

It seemed the sheriff's department was at the Springs Apartment more than any other location outside the office. Shar pulled in front of the leasing office. They might as well rent an apartment and take up residence.

Holden lived on the far end, second story. "Stay alert," Shar told the deputy. "We aren't liked very much in this complex."

"I wouldn't think so." He motioned to a drunk slumped under a bush. "Drugs, drinking, and prostitution would be my guess."

"They stick to themselves, mostly, but I'm out here at least twice a month for some man beating on his girl." She kept her hand close to her weapon and knocked on Holden's door. "Sheriff."

The door swung open. "What did that piece of crap say I did now?" A disheveled young man in dire need of a shower glared at them.

"Roger Holden?"

"Yeah."

"We're here to ask you some questions about Lacey Tales. May we come in?" Shar pushed past him.

"Hey. Whatever." He shrugged and closed the door behind them. "I kicked Lori and her brat out earlier this month. Except for her crying at my door an hour or so ago, I ain't seen either one of them."

"So, you are aware the child is missing?" Shar raised her eyebrows.

"Lori told me." His eyes widened. "You mean that wasn't a ploy to get me to take her back?"

"Unfortunately, no."

He plopped onto a torn armchair. "Wow. I liked that little girl."

"Well enough to kick them to the streets," Pinson muttered.

"Lori started…uh, selling tricks to pay the rent. I can't have that here. I'm doing my best to keep clean. My probation officer shows up all the time. If he found out I was living with a prostitute, he'd send me back to jail."

"What were you incarcerated for?"

"Dealing." He sighed and rubbed his hands against the faded brown whiskers on his cheeks. "What can I do to help?"

"Ask around. Keep your eyes open." Shar handed him a business card. "Call us if you find out anything." She pivoted on her heel and exited the apartment.

"Do you think he knows anything?" Pinson asked, once they were out of earshot of the apartment.

"No." Even though Shar retained her "sheriff" mask of impassiveness on her face as they made their way to the jeep, she kept her wits about her and her eyes open.

If not, she wouldn't have seen the three-year-old boy slip through a child-sized hole in the pool gate.

Shar tried the gate to find it locked. "Don't go close to the water, sweetie." She glanced at the sharp spikes on the top of the fence. With a tired groan, she grabbed ahold, launching herself over. The loud tear of material alerted her to the fact she'd ripped her only clean pair of uniform pants. "Get a key to let us out," she told Pinson.

The child glanced back and fell in.

Shar reached down, grabbed the little boy by the hair and pulled him to the surface. "I got you." Anchoring her hands under his arms, she pulled him out of the pool and stared into his face. "You're alright. Where's Mommy?"

He glanced upward.

"Of course, she is." Shar held tight to his hand. "Let's go give her a piece of my mind, shall we?"

The moment a harried leasing manager unlocked the pool gate, Shar headed for the child's apartment. "Get the fence fixed now," she told the manager, "or I'm arresting you for child neglect."

Shar hefted the child to her hip and marched to his apartment. The door hung open. A woman sprawled on the sofa. "Is that your mommy?"

"Mommy." The boy squirmed to be let down.

An empty whiskey bottle sat on the scarred coffee table. An untied silk robe showed the woman wore nothing else.

Shar lifted her radio from her belt and called child protective services. She closed the apartment door and grabbed a grocery bag from the floor. "Show me your room, buddy."

He thundered to the one and only bedroom. "Teddy." The child snatched a tattered teddy bear and clutched it to his chest.

Shar pulled articles of little boy clothing, some pull-ups, and a threadbare blanket. "Let's go, Brian. Is that your name?" She pointed to a plaque with the name.

"Yep." He nodded so hard his curls bounced.

Shar took his hand and headed for the door.

"What's happening?" The mother sat up on the sofa.

"Is this your son?"

She blinked bleary eyes. "Yeah."

"Child Protective Services are on their way. Brian is coming with me. Have a good day." Shar opened the door. "Your little boy was seconds away from drowning. Good thing I happened along, huh?" She stepped out and slammed the door against the woman's protests.

"Fierce." Pinson grinned.

"Some people don't deserve children." She hoisted the child in the backseat of her jeep, hooked the seatbelt tightly around him, and vowed to buy a car seat to keep handy. The last thing she needed was for CPS to come knocking on her door.

CHAPTER TWO

The Child Saver watched the group of day care children traipse past her on the sidewalk, holding onto a knotted rope like obedient puppies. She had a buyer for a dark-haired little boy. Little Lacey had fetched a pretty penny and would soon be at her new home in California. Now, who to choose…

She stepped forward as a little boy let go of the rope, but halted when the childcare worker turned. She smiled at The Child Saver, then transferred her attention to the child.

"Don't let go, Brian. I've told you before." She glanced back up. "There are usually two of us, but my partner is out with the flu. It's our weekly visit to the library for story time. Could you help?"

"Of course." It couldn't be more perfect. The Child Saver grasped the end of the rope and followed along. So many beautiful children, but only one or two needed saving if the state of their clothing was any indication.

"No, no, Brian. Keep a hold." She covered his chubby hand with hers over the rope when he let go for the third time.

"Poor thing is a foster child and has no idea of what we're doing," the worker said. "But, he'll learn. He's a bright little boy."

Just what The Child Saver needed. She grinned and put a bounce in her step. She'd call her helper, Amy, the first chance she had a free moment. The boy needed taking, and The Child Saver had to go to work.

* * *

"I still say if neither one of us is getting married any time soon, we should adopt." Candy crossed her ankles and propped her feet on the porch railing. "We're running out of time to be parents."

Shar couldn't deny that she'd thought of it. "My job keeps me too busy. Besides, I have this big fur baby right here." She scratched Goliath behind the ear.

"Mine doesn't, and a dog isn't the same." She took a sip of her wine. "I'm seriously considering it, Shar. I'll be thirty-nine soon, and I want to be a mother."

Shar smiled, thinking of Brian. Dark curls and eyes just like Everis. No. She wouldn't think of Everis, but if she were to adopt, she would want Brian. Maybe she would. Then her child and Candy's would grow up together. She lifted her wineglass. "Let's do this." They clinked glass and laughed.

Locusts hummed from the woods surrounding the house. A slight breeze blew strands of Shar's hair around her face, some sticking to the lip gloss on her lips. The sun was setting over the horizon, illuminating the car parked at the end of the driveway and the man, who was striding toward them with a long-legged gait she recognized. Goliath stood and wagged his tail.

"That man gets better looking every time I see him." Candy stood. "I'll leave you alone to shout at him or shoot him. Whichever you prefer."

Everis, hair a little longer, the shadow of a beard gracing his strong chin, stopped at the bottom of the steps. "Hello, Shar."

She had to clear her throat before she said, "Everis. It's been a while."

"May I sit?" He motioned toward the chair Candy had vacated.

She nodded and resumed her seat, using the wineglass to her lips as an opportunity to gain her composure. "What brings you back?"

"I volunteered." His teeth flashed.

She refused to be swayed by his charm. "Oh? Follow another killer to our town?"

"Not a killer, per se." He reached for her hand, persisting when she pulled away. "Please, I'm sorry I haven't called. I've been undercover in South America, and couldn't risk exposure."

She took a deep, shuddering breath. "I know. I'm sorry I'm acting like a spoiled housewife."

"Glad to know you missed me."

She smiled. "Who are you here for?"

"You."

"Work-wise, smarty pants." A warm flush filled her.

"I'm looking for someone kidnapping and selling children. Have you heard of the disappearances in Missouri over last year?"

"Of course."

"We think the child that disappeared here may be connected."

"Why do you think that?"

He straightened and propped his feet on the railing.

"Someone saw Lacey Tales' picture on the news. Even with her hair dyed dark, the woman recognized her. Turns out it's the neighbor of the couple who paid big bucks for a little girl of their own."

"Good news."

He nodded. "They described the woman who sold the child as a Hispanic woman of small stature and limited English."

Shar finished her wine. "Want a glass?"

"Beer?"

"Sure thing. I'll be right back." Shar moved to the kitchen. Was the woman who sold Lacey working alone or was she the gopher of the adoption scheme? She snagged a beer from the fridge and poured herself another glass of wine before returning to Everis. "Did the couple visit a sketch artist?"

"Yeah, but I'm not holding out much hope. The sketch is very generic." He pulled a folded piece of paper from his shirt pocket and handed it to Shar. "Look familiar?"

She studied the petite features of a woman with dark hair piled on top of her head, dark eyes, a large nose, and thin lips. "Could be almost any middle-aged woman. We haven't had another child disappear, Everis. Maybe the ring isn't operating out of Highland Springs."

"What's your poverty rate?"

"Less than half." She tilted her head. "Are you telling me they only take low-income children?"

"That's what it seems like, and the Ozarks are full of them." He leaned forward, letting his hands dangle between his knees. "I'm here to work the case with you."

Her mask slipped into place. Not that Everis blamed her. Maybe he should have risked finding a way to let her know he hadn't forgotten about her. But, his going undercover had resulted in bringing down a drug ring operating out of Texarkana. "Are you opposed to working with me?"

"Why should I be?" She stood and moved to the railing, staring out across the lawn. "I'm for finding justice, same as you."

He followed and wrapped his arms around her. "I really did miss you."

"I missed you, too." She shifted to face him. "Very much. So, now what?"

"We pick up where we left off." He lowered his head and claimed her lips in a kiss.

Fire burned in his gut. No one felt or tasted quite like Shar. He pulled away and rested his forehead against hers. "I could do that for the rest of my life."

"Hold that thought." She pulled her cell phone from her pocket and lifted it to her ear. "Sheriff Camenetti." She listened for a moment, then hung up. "We have a missing child. That's the second one this month."

"Let's go. I'll drive." He glanced at the beer can. He'd have to enjoy it later.

Shar disappeared into the house, returning within five minutes in her uniform, gun belt around her waist. She sniffed and rushed past him down the porch steps.

"You're crying, why?" He chased after her.

"It's a little boy named Brian. I want to adopt him."

He hadn't expected that answer. He glanced over as he slid into the driver's seat of his rented car. "Adoption. Wow. Okay. We'll revisit this topic later."

Everis had always wanted a child of his own, and lately those dreams had included Shar. He knew she was in her middle thirties. Maybe she thought herself too old.

Shar directed him to an upper middle-class neighborhood. "Third house on the left."

He pulled into the driveway where a couple around his age stood with five other children surrounding them. Snatching a flashlight from the glove compartment, he glanced at Shar. "Foster parents?"

"Yes. Handpicked by me. Mr. and Mrs. Simpson." She shoved open her door and strode toward them.

"We're sorry, Sheriff." The man put his arm around the woman. "The children were playing in the backyard before bath time, when Logan said Brian was missing. The gate is still shut."

Everis glanced around the house. A five-foot chain-link enclosed the yard. "It wouldn't be hard for someone to reach over and grab a lightweight child. The other children didn't hear or see anything?"

"No, sir."

"Is it possible he climbed over?" Everis felt certain the child had been taken, but wouldn't exhaust hope just yet.

"It's possible. He does get into things."

"I'll take the alley from the west end." Shar took off at a sprint.

That left the east end for Everis. "Mr. Simpson, you should send your family inside and patrol the streets. You know this little one better than we do." He rushed to the end of the street.

Once there, he turned on the flashlight. Far ahead Shar's light flickered.

He kept the light trained on the ground, searching

for a piece of fabric, a footprint, a spot of blood. He reached the Simpson yard the same time Shar did. "Nothing."

"Me either," she said. "Oh, Everis, he's the sweetest little boy."

He encompassed her hand in his large one, then gently squeezed it. "We'll find him. Just like Lacey, someone will find him."

She nodded and exhaled deeply. She peered more closely at the top of the fence and wiped something with her finger. "Shine your light on this."

He did, revealing a red smudge. "Blood?"

"Which means Brian could be injured." She circled toward him. "No other signs. They would have had to have a car parked nearby."

"Would the child have cried or screamed?" Everis kept close by her side.

"I don't think so. When I found him in the apartment complex, he went with me without a fuss." She knelt and focused her light on a set of tire tracks. "We need to check these against residents who share this alley."

"Got it." He dialed Mayfield's number.

"Hey, stranger. You back?" Mayfield's sleepy voice came on the line.

"I'm here to help with the serial kidnappers. We need you to come to the address I'll text you and be prepared to get tire casts of a set in the alley and compare to neighbors'."

"Oh, yay. Be there in fifteen." Click.

Shar gave a wry grin. "He hates to be awakened. Good thing is—he'll wake up Pinson, who hates it even more." She stood and started following the tracks.

"They end at the pavement."

"We caught Lars; we'll catch these people, too." He quirked his mouth. "We make a formidable team."

"Right, crooks, killers, and kidnappers beware." She headed back to the Simpson house.

The family had disappeared inside, the family van gone. Good. Mr. Simpson had followed Everis's suggestion to go searching. It would give the man something to do besides sitting home and worrying.

After taking a formal statement, and doing their best to provide comfort to the frightened foster mother, Everis drove Shar home. He walked her to the steps, then stopped. "Do you really want to adopt this child?"

She searched. "Yes. Why?"

"No reason, really. I just never thought about adoption."

"He looks just like you. Three years old with dark hair and eyes." She sighed and faced the house. "Goodnight, Everis."

Three years old. Ice water poured through Everis's veins. He reached out to stop Shar from climbing the stairs. "Who is his mother?"

Her eyes widened. "No," she whispered.

He gripped her shoulders. "I need to know her name."

"Brianna Wilson."

He couldn't breathe. His heart threatened to pound from his chest. Three years ago, Everis had been in a dark place. Drinking and women filled every minute he wasn't working. "I need to go. I'll see you in the morning." He dashed for his car.

"Everis!"

Ignoring her cry, he climbed into the driver's seat

and sped off, tires squealing against the road. Things just became a whole lot hotter.

CYNTHIA HICKEY

CHAPTER THREE

Everis parked in front of the complex and made his way to Brianna Wilson's apartment. His hand trembled as he knocked sharply. He couldn't believe this was happening. From the pit of despair to being on top of his game, now this.

More beaten down, but still pretty, Brianna opened the door. Long dark curls tangled around a face sagging from a hard life. She blinked several times, then smiled. "Evie."

"Don't call me that." He pushed his way into the apartment, then put his hands on her shoulders and forced her to focus on him. "Is your son mine?"

"What? Did you bring him back? That mean sheriff took him away."

"Answer me." He shook her. "Is the child mine?"

She drew in a long breath through her nose. "Yes."

"Why didn't you tell me?" He released her, running his hands through his hair as he paced the small room.

"At first, I couldn't find you. Then, I moved here because you were here. Then, you left again." With a trembling hand, she lit a cigarette. "You're a hard man to keep track of." She narrowed her eyes. "The way I

19

see it, you owe me three years of back child support."

"You'll get it, but Brian is mine. He won't step foot near you again." He waved a hand around the dirty apartment.

Dishes overflowed from the sink to the counter. Filled ashtrays littered every available surface. Marijuana paraphernalia lay scattered across the coffee table, and empty liquor bottles lay at random angles below it.

"You aren't fit to be a mother."

She shrugged. "Way I remember it, you weren't much better."

"I am now. You'll get a check in the mail. Don't look me up, don't try and see Brian."

She ducked her head. "You think you can find him?"

"I'll do everything in my power." He slammed the door behind him. Outside, he leaned against the door and closed his eyes. He had a son. Someone had kidnapped his son. Shar wanted to adopt same son. He swallowed past the lump forming in his throat. Late hour or not, he had to return to Shar's and tell her.

His mind whirled on the way. Just the suspicion of him having a child had put a shadow of pain in her eyes. Now, he had to tell her what he'd suspected was true. Brianna had no reason to lie. Shar had said the boy looked just like him. He pounded a hand on the steering wheel. Where was the child?

Shar stepped onto her porch the moment he pulled into her driveway and cut the lights. They stared at each other for several minutes before she nodded and waved him forward.

The walk up to her house felt like the final walk

from death row to the gas chamber must feel like. Would she send him away or wait until after they found Brian before giving him the boot?

"Is he yours?" She asked before he sat down.

"Yes."

"How do you feel about it?"

"Which part?" He sat in the chair next to her and reached for her hand. Surprisingly, she allowed him to entwine his fingers with hers. "The part where I just found out I'm a father or the part where some maniac has kidnapped, and probably sold, my son? I'm numb."

"This is my turn to promise." She squeezed his hand. "We'll get him back."

He shook his head and gazed into her eyes. "I'm going to hold onto that promise." He tugged on her hand until her face was close. "I'm sorry. I wasn't the same person three or four years ago."

"We've all made mistakes, Everis." She cupped his face with her free hand. "He's an adorable little boy, despite his mother."

He pulled her head toward him and kissed her, long and deep, expressing with his lips what he couldn't say with words.

* • •

The Child Saver stared down at the sleeping boy. Why hadn't anyone clicked on his photo yet? He was such a handsome child.

She twirled a finger in one of his curls. "Perhaps, I'll keep you," she whispered. "I'll take you with me when I leave this place. Why not? I've provided children to many others. Why not keep you for myself?"

She stretched out on the bed beside him and pulled

him close. He made little sounds in his sleep, and she smiled. "I'm calling you Devin. Maybe, I'll find you a sister before I quit. We're quite rich, son. We can leave soon."

Yes, they were rich, but the money was so easy to come by, and there were so many children to be saved. Still, Highland Springs would be her last hunting ground. She'd head to the coast and raise her children in the sun and sand. Devin and Darcy. She'd find a Darcy easily enough.

Since tomorrow was Sunday, The Child Saver had an entire day to spend with Devon and hunt for more beautiful children to be adopted.

After a healthy breakfast of scrambled eggs and bacon, though Devin only nibbled at a strip of bacon, The Child Saver loaded him into her van and headed up the mountain. The morning hadn't started well since her son refused to eat his eggs. Now, the sun sat high in the sky making it easier for anyone paying attention to see them.

She cruised the one road of a blink-and-you'll-miss-it town. When she spotted a shack with a dirt yard filled with young children, she slowed and did a U-turn, then pressed the button on an old tape recorder. Within seconds, the tinny sound of ice cream-truck music drifted through the window.

She grinned as the children toddled toward her. She'd hit pay dirt. Five children ranging from age one to five. Their mother must have been a busy woman. Obviously, she couldn't care for them properly.

Opening the side door, she waved them in with promises of candy and other treats. The oldest child hefted a baby on her tiny hip. Who in their right mind allowed a child of five to babysit? The Child Saver was doing a very good thing that day.

* * *

After a restless night of flitting in and out of dreams and nightmares, Shar carried a cardboard carrier of coffee down the sidewalk to the sheriff's office. She could have driven, but the conversation with Everis of the night before still swirled through her brain. It didn't matter to her that he had a child. What kept her awake was the shock that the child she wanted was his.

She glanced up to see her jeep barreling toward her. Everis stopped and rolled down the passenger window. "Drop those and get in. We've had an entire family snatched not thirty minutes ago."

Shar spun toward a passing woman and handed her the drinks, minus hers and Everis's. "Please take these to my office. I'd appreciate it." She handed Everis a steaming cup of coffee through the window, then climbed into the passenger seat. "These people are brave."

"Balls the size of a water tower." He pressed the gas and rocketed them out of town.

A few drops of Shar's coffee splashed out and onto her hand. She licked them off, grateful she preferred blended over hot. "How many? What ages?"

"Five. Ages one to six. The six-year-old is small for her age, the mother said. Which makes sense, considering these people don't usually take children over five."

"Because the younger ones are easier to control?" She glanced over.

"Because adoptee parents want young, is my guess."

Half an hour later, they headed up the mountain and stopped in front of a small house. A harried woman, so thin a strong wind would blow her away, ran toward them. "They're all gone. Every single one." She collapsed in the dirt.

Everis and Shar reached her at the same time.

Everis helped her to her feet and into the house while Shar glanced around the yard. A balding doll lay in a tiny patch of grass, next to a half-empty bottle. Several matchbox cars were scattered around, making the area a landmine for anyone with bare feet. It was easy to see children lived there.

How had they been taken without anyone seeing? Two other houses faced the street. They weren't close as the homes in town were, but they weren't isolated either. Shar headed to the nearest one.

The curtains fell into place as she approached the house. Shar knocked. No one answered. "It's Sheriff Camenetti. I'd like to speak to you, please. I know you're in there."

The door opened a crack, and a wrinkled face peered out. "No reason for you to be here."

Shar rolled her head on her neck to get the kinks out and let her sheriff mask fall into place. "Ma'am, I'm afraid I wouldn't be here without reason. I can ask you questions out here if you'd rather I didn't come in." Then, she'd get a warrant and search the place thoroughly.

"Ask them right now. I can hear you."

Shar sighed. "Five children are missing."

"The ones from across the street? That's too bad, although that woman ain't fit to take care of a dog."

"Why do you say that?"

"After her husband died, she's lived off welfare and the kindness of others. Now, me...when my husband died, I took care of myself."

By staying cloistered in her house. "Did you see anything suspicious within the hour? Hear anything out of the ordinary?"

"Why, yes." The door opened another inch. "I heard an ice cream truck playing "Pop Goes the Weasel." Ice cream trucks never come down this road. Ain't nobody got money for such luxuries around here. Oh, and I saw a silver van headed up the road, then turned and came back. Never did see the ice cream truck, but I know I heard one."

"Thank you. You've been a big help."

The door closed.

The next house didn't see a van, but they did hear the ice cream music. Was it possible the kidnapper lured kids toward the van that way?

Shar fished her phone from her pocket and called the Simpsons.

"No, none of us heard one of those. Remember, it was already dark when Brian was taken." The woman's voice broke. "If an ice cream truck had been anywhere close, these children would have been clamoring for a dollar."

"Thank you." Shar hung up and met up with Everis next to her jeep. "We need to find out if anyone in Missouri claims to have heard an ice cream truck." She explained about her conversations. "How's the mother?"

"Frantic. Her kids are all she has left." He moved to the passenger side of the jeep, letting Shar drive. "Mayfield called and said there's no match on the tire tread in the alley other than it matches tires commonly used on minivans."

"Well, a silver van was spotted around the time of the children's disappearance. We may have gotten our first real clue." She drove them back to the office.

Everis tacked photos of the children alongside Lacey Tales, and Brian. Seven children taken in less than two weeks.

Shar groaned. It was time to call the media and alert the public. She really needed to hire someone who didn't mind being on camera, because she hated it. "Hey, Everis, do you mind being on TV?"

Chapter Four

Two of the five siblings were spoken for, both of them girls. The Child Saver decided to keep the infant. As she watched it throw food from its high chair, she wondered whether she shouldn't have kept one of the older girls. Babies fetched top dollar. "Stop that, Darcy. Bad girl."

The baby opened her mouth and wailed.

"Amy! Get your lazy butt in here and help me. I have to go to work. Ugh." A dollop of the baby's oatmeal flew through the air and landed on The Child Saver's sweater. "I'm selling this child and finding another one to keep. I can't do the baby thing." She shouldered her purse and stormed out of the house and into her new shiny, black Mercedes. One of the few luxuries she'd allowed herself from her profits.

On the way to work, she smiled and waved. Several people stopped to stare. Oh, right, her cover was a dour woman in this town. She'd been friendly in the last. So much to remember. She'd practically forgotten who she really was anymore.

* * *

"There's the sheriff, boys. I'm sure she'll have

something to say about your shenanigans."

Shar turned to see the librarian, Dorothy Mayfield, brandishing a book at a group of nine-year-olds. That woman complained more than any other female in town. If you didn't like people...oh, that's probably why she worked as a librarian. She rarely had to talk to anyone.

"What's going on?" Shar tossed her empty coffee cup in a nearby trashcan.

"These, these, boys." Ms. Mayfield shook a book in her face. "Thought it funny to tear out the dirty pictures and make paper airplanes with them. Someone is going to pay for this."

Shar held out her hand. Mercy. The Art of Kamasutra. Those boys got an education. Shar's face heated. "Shouldn't this be in a restricted area, or something?"

"Are you telling me how to do my job, Sheriff?" Ms. Mayfield crossed her arms.

"Not at all. These boys will definitely pay for the book. Follow me, guys. We're calling your parents from the office. I'm sure they will be very disappointed in you."

"Not if we say we were almost stolen." A dark-haired boy with a face full of freckles glared up at her. "Then, we'll have their sympathy."

"Were you almost stolen?" Shar narrowed her eyes. "Because if you say you were, but weren't, then I can add lying to a police officer to your list of crimes."

"What list?"

"The one I'm making right now." She pointed to the door of the sheriff's office. "March. Single file."

"What's this?" Everis asked, glancing up from a

28

stack of papers on the conference table.

Shar flipped the caseboard around so the kids couldn't see. "These boys destroyed a library book and learned a whole lot about adult matters. They need to call home before I feed them to Goliath."

The boys drew back as Goliath circled the table and stared at them. The dog wouldn't hurt them, but they didn't need to know Goliath was nothing more than a teddy bear.

Everis slid the phone in their direction. "No funny stuff. Call your parents and have them come here. They'll have to sign you out." He glanced at Shar and winked.

The agent would make a fine father. Kind, caring, and fair. *Lord, help us get Brian back.* So far there hadn't been even a tiny sign of his location. The strain wore on Everis in the slump of his shoulders and the lines around his eyes.

Once all four of the boys had called their parents, the screaming over the phone having reached the whole room, they sat along the wall, staring at their shoes with dejected faces.

Amber stuck her head in and handed Shar a slip of paper. "The cost of the book."

"Thirty-five dollars?"

"That's $8.75 per kid." Amber flashed a grin and tottered out on her stilettos.

"Who knew she was a math whiz?" Everis focused back on the papers in front of him.

"Just because she looks dumb doesn't mean she is. Eyes back in your heads, boys." Shar snapped her fingers.

Four heads jerked back down and away from where

Amber had disappeared. Good grief. With hormones like those at eleven, what were they going to be like at thirteen?

The parents arrived, angry and embarrassed, with promises to pay their share of the library book and take the money out of their son's hide. Shar smiled as they left with their delinquents. "I wish that was the worst we had to deal with around here."

"Me, too." Everis stood. "Want to pay a visit to the library with me? I'd like to look at some old maps."

"What are you thinking?"

"That Highland Springs, or somewhere close, might be the center of decades of child abductions."

Shar's eyes widened. "You think it's a family...thing?"

He shrugged. "Maybe. I've been doing some browsing on the internet, but the files only go back so far back. These abductions aren't a new thing for these parts; they're happening with a higher frequency. I want to read through some books on this area's history, and Mayfield said the library had some."

At least they were doing something. Sitting around twiddling their thumbs, waiting for something to break on the case wouldn't find Brian or the others. They'd done a press conference, flashing the faces of the missing children across the television, put out an APB on a gray minivan, and put up fliers in every store down Main Street. Someone, somewhere, must know something. They just had to find that someone.

Mayfield and Pinson entered the conference room, returning from yet another fight at The Springs apartment. Pinson raised his eyebrows in Everis's direction. "You got a kid?"

Everis stiffened, then met the deputy's stare. "Appears so."

"The boy that's missing."

Everis exhaled heavily. "How do you know this?"

"We just arrested your baby mama." Pinson grinned. "Prostitution. Maybe the kid isn't yours."

Everis shot to his feet. "I guess we'll find out when we bring the boy home, won't we, deputy?"

"Stand down, Pinson." Shar shook her head. "You're out of line."

"It's good to know the high and mighty Agent Hayes is human."

Shar motioned to a stack of messages. "Take care of those. When you've finished, go online and search where a person can find a child on the black market."

"You're assigning me desk duty?" His face darkened.

"Yep." She grinned and brushed past him. "Coming, Agent Hayes?" She snapped her fingers for Goliath to follow.

* * *

"I didn't need you to take up for me." Everis caught up with Shar.

"I know, but as the sheriff, the deputies are my responsibility, and Pinson needed taking down a notch or two. Do you want to speak with Ms. Wilson before we leave?"

"Just long enough to find out why she was brought in."

"I'll wait outside." Shar moved outside as Everis headed for the holding cell.

He peered through the small window. Brianna sat slumped over, clearly intoxicated. Mascara tracks marred her cheeks. Torn jeans and a skimpy top completed the ensemble. He pressed the button to enter.

Brianna opened one eye, then straightened. "Are you here to let me out?"

"Nope." He stared down at her. "Why don't you stop this life and clean up your act? You have a son."

"Not anymore." She hung her head. "That sheriff took him away, then he was lost."

"I'll get him back." He squatted in front of her. "I'm going to get custody if I prove he's mine."

She jerked up. Her eyes flashed. "He is. I wouldn't lie about that."

"If you ever want to see him, Bri, you have to clean up your act. If not for him, for you." He pulled a check from his pocket. "Here's a thousand dollars. I'll give you more later. You can use it to post bail or not. Your choice." He stood, dropping the check on the bench beside her.

"Thank you."

Why he felt compelled to help her was a mystery. He'd never loved her. She had only been someone to share a dark time with. Heck, he'd probably never even liked her. That made him the same scum she was. He motioned for Amber to unlock the door, then stepped out. The woman he loved waited for him outside. The question now was...could she love him in return, knowing the type of past he'd had?

He couldn't change anything. Best to move on and show her the man he now was. He pushed through the front door.

Shar leaned against the front of her jeep and stared down the street. From the blank look in her eyes, she wasn't seeing anything, just lost in her thoughts. She jumped when his foot sent a rock clattering across her path. "Oh. Ready?"

"Yep." He climbed into the passenger seat and fastened his seatbelt. "That woman is a lost cause," he said when Shar got in.

"No one is ever a lost cause." She started the jeep and turned toward the library.

She parked in front, ordering Goliath to stay, and rolled down the windows. "He's been trained not to leave unless I call him."

"Good." Everis remembered the time the dog had inadvertently alerted The Silencer to their presence. "Does he have a command?"

"Come." She grinned and opened the door, commanding the dog to stay when he tried to follow.

They walked side by side into the library as if they'd worked together as partners their entire career. What would it be like to work with her every day and not just when something really bad happened in Highland Springs?

The librarian, a sour-faced old woman who'd practically kicked them out of the building a year ago, glanced up with a scowl. "What now?"

Everis flashed a grin. "Please direct us to the history of Highland Springs."

The woman pointed and returned to whatever she was looking at on her computer. Her scowl deepened at whatever she was looking at. When she caught Everis watching, she shifted the screen further away from him.

"Have a good day, Miss." He winked and followed Shar to the section of reference books. "That is a strange old bird."

"We like to say she's got character." Shar smiled

and pulled down a thick dusty volume. "This one might be what we're looking for." She carried the book to a nearby table.

Everis scooted a chair close to her side as she opened the book. He scanned page after page until reaching the section on the Great Depression. There he read of families who couldn't afford to feed their children and sent them to a children's home, thinking the move would be temporary. Instead, the children were given new names and adopted out. After the depression, when families were more financially secure, children disappeared from their homes, school, playgrounds. "This is scary."

Shar nodded and flipped faster through the pages. "There's nothing more."

"Until now, that is." Everis straightened. "Is there anyone left in town who would have been alive back then?"

Shar sucked her bottom lip between her teeth, something she did when in deep thought. The simple gesture made Everis's mouth dry up. He couldn't pull is gaze from her lips, the desire to kiss her strong.

She said something he didn't hear.

"I'm sorry. What?"

"Mr. Melson. He's ninety-five years old and still lives alone up on the mountain. We'll have to be careful. He usually shoots at visitors."

Chapter Five

Nosy busybodies. The Child Saver watched as the sheriff and the agent passed. If they kept interfering in her quest to save the little ones, she'd have to make them pay.

"Amy, bring me my children and a big glass of wine. I've had a bad day." She sat in her recliner, put her feet up, and turned on the television. Hopefully, there would be no more cries for help in finding the missing children. She'd just managed to get rid of all but the two she kept.

Amy set Darcy on her lap. "Devin is still eating."

"How long?"

"Half an hour."

The Child Saver frowned. "He's had more than enough time. He comes to me or he sits in the closet. His choice."

The brat ended up sitting in the closet. Why he would prefer the dark over her soft lap was beyond her comprehension. Other than crying at the slightest provocation, Darcy had turned into the least trouble of the two.

"But that's alright. Mummy loves you." She hugged

the girl, breathing in the scent of...milk? "Amy!"

The woman bustled to her side. "Yes?"

"Why does this child smell like sour milk?"

"She spilled some earlier and—"

The Child Saver thrust the girl at her. "Give her a bath and refill my wine." The woman was slacking in her duties. If she couldn't keep up her part of the job, she'd have to be replaced.

Shar parked at the end of Mr. Melson's drive and focused on the door through the front windshield. Sure enough, the barrel of a gun greeted them before a man, so thin he could stand sideways and disappear, stepped onto the porch.

"Move on out."

She rolled her window down. "Sheriff."

"I don't care who you are. I don't want visitors."

Goliath showed his big head through Shar's window. "Back, boy."

"You got a bear in there?"

"No, sir, just a dog."

"In that case, come on up. I like dogs." He lowered his shotgun and took a seat in a wooden rocking chair.

"Is it safe?" Everis asked, peering intently at the man.

"He's more bark than bite. A person just has to wait to be invited." Shar climbed out and opened the back door. "Come, Goliath. Go make a friend."

The dog trotted by her side until they reached the steps, then climbed on the seat to sit next to Mr. Melson.

"You're a handsome lad, aren't you?" A smile spread across the wrinkled face. "Alright, Sheriff, I'll bite. Why are you here?"

She joined him and leaned against the railing as Everis stood on the top step. "This is Agent Hayes. He's here helping the department find out who is taking the children of Highland Springs."

"Children?" He paled. "I ain't got a TV. Don't listen to the news. You'll have to explain." He put a thick veined hand on Goliath's head.

Shar explained everything that had happened since Lacey's disappearance. "We're hoping you might remember something about when this same thing happened over eighty years ago."

"I do. I was ten, and my little sister was one of the taken." He set his chair to rocking. "That was a bad time for this town. Twelve children disappeared. We never saw any of them again."

"Who ran the home?"

"A couple by the name of Smith. People as common as their name. Unfriendly, but seemed to take care of the children, until they started selling them."

"What happened to the Smiths?" Shar glanced at Everis.

"They took off one night when the feds were on their tail. Rumor is they adopted one of the girls for their own and took her with them."

"Did anyone see this girl?"

"I did, once. At least I think it was her. She had dark hair and eyes. Plain little thing. Sad, too." He gave a deep sigh. "I hate to think this is happening again. The sheriff back then, your grandpa, worked himself to death trying to find those kids. I hope you succeed where he failed."

"I plan on it." The people of Highland Springs

depended on her. Last time, it had been young women being murdered. This time, parents were frantic over the loss of their babies. Shar wouldn't let them down.

"Thank you for your time, Mr. Melson." Shar offered her hand.

He gave a firm shake. "I voted for you. Don't let me down."

"We won't." Everis stepped forward and shook the man's hand when Shar stepped back. "Please call the office if you remember anything else."

"Will do, son." The man stared past them, his hand back on the dog's head. "I didn't think I'd live long enough to see such an atrocity again." He closed his eyes and was snoring within seconds.

"Come, Goliath." Shar patted her thigh and headed back to the jeep. Smith was as common as Jones for a last name. Dark-haired and dark-eyed children were just as common. "I know where the old home stands. It's abandoned, so I doubt we'd find anything useful, but it's worth a look."

The Highland Springs Home for Children sat on the edge of town in an area now quickly turning to commercial buildings. Shar had always hoped someone would convert the old Victorian into something useful again. With chipped paint, broken windows, and a yard high with weeds, the house resembled a scab on a never-healing wound.

"This must have been beautiful once upon a time. When was the last time someone lived here?" Everis lifted and moved the sagging gate.

"A woman and her daughter lived here about thirty years ago, I think. I was pretty young and don't remember much except that the woman would have been maybe twenty-five, her daughter an infant. The child's father took it one day and fled. The woman left soon after."

"Were they positive it was the child's father?"

"That's what my mother always told me. She said he'd left a note stating the mother was unfit to raise a child. No one ever contested the fact." She followed him to the sagging front porch.

"Strange how things come full circle." He gently pushed open the front door. It squeaked on its hinges. "Families wanting to do better for their children lost something precious, a young mother loses her child to someone who thought he was better, children are disappearing again, and I find out the mother of my child is unfit."

Wow. Shar hadn't thought it through as thoroughly, but the commonalities chilled her to the bone. Talk about sins of the fathers, or mothers. "Sometimes, I think Highland Springs is cursed."

Everis was inclined to agree with her. The last two cases had started outside Highland Springs, but came to fruition in the small mountain town. While he regretted the reason for coming to town, he held a glimmer of gratitude for the opportunity to meet Shar. He'd never met anyone like her before.

The door opened onto a cavernous front hall with a sweeping staircase as a focal point. Off to his right was a parlor containing a large rock fireplace. To his left, a dining room that could easily hold a table big enough for twenty. "This must have been some place once upon a time."

Shar ran her hand over a rickety newel post. "I wish

it could be restored, but with shops building up around it, it isn't likely."

"Maybe the historical society could do something."

She grinned. "Maybe. I'll bring it up at the town meeting. It would make a beautiful museum and visitor center."

"It would." Everis opened a small door under the staircase. Cobwebs and dust made their home there now. He ran his hand over the narrow shelves. His fingers closed over a small metal object. "Found a key."

"To what?"

"No idea." He straightened and brushed webs from his hair. "Let's keep looking. Who owns this place?"

She shrugged. "I guess the mother I remember, or maybe her daughter. Since no one remembers their names or where they went, maybe there's a record of foreclosure. I'll check into it."

Everis moved through the dining room and into the kitchen, running his hands over the walls. It wasn't unheard of for old homes to have hidden passages, and if they were smuggling children in and out, they'd need secret tunnels. He swiveled and stared at the fireplace. Something had seemed off at first glance.

"Shar, does this fireplace seem abnormally clean to you?" No black soot stained the stones. He expected it to be dusty from sitting for so many years, but to not be marred by smoke…

"It doesn't look as if it's ever been used." She knelt on the mantle and placed her hands on the back. A sharp click and the back swung open. "Clever."

"Let me go first." Everis waited for her to back up, then crawled through the space into a small room. Bunkbeds lined the walls. A makeshift curtain hung around a bucket with a toilet seat on top. What a horrible place to stash children.

"Oh." Shar joined him. "This is awful. I hope the children today are held somewhere better than this."

So did Everis. The thought of Brian sleeping in a cave with dirt walls made him cringe.

At the back of the room was a wooden door. Through that a tunnel. Shar unclipped a flashlight from her belt and handed it to him. "Let's see where this goes. My guess is it comes out somewhere in the woods."

"That's what…a mile?" He turned on the light and shined it around the walls and ceilings. Thick beams held the earth at bay. "I hope it doesn't cave in. No one knows we're here."

"I texted Mayfield. I do that every time I head off on my own."

"That's what I like about you. You think ahead."

She laughed. "Stop with the compliments and get moving."

He gave her hand a squeeze, then, not letting go, proceeded, hoping and praying, the path wouldn't lead to their grave. "I hate dark, closed-in places."

"I'm here with you."

He swallowed past the lump in his throat and wiped his sleeve across his perspiring brow. He could do this. He had to do this.

"Concentrate on breathing slow and deep," Shar said. "I can hear you, and you're breathing too fast. We can back out, and I'll come back with one of the deputies."

"Don't be ridiculous. We're already here." One…two…three…he was in hell. Four…Five…he couldn't get enough air. He released Shar's hand and bent over, hands braced on his knees.

"No. We aren't doing this. Come on." She grabbed his arm and practically dragged him back to the house. "Sit." She pointed to a dusty chair. "I'm calling Mayfield."

"No. Just give me a minute. I didn't think the tunnel would be that long."

"It is." She knelt in front of him, keeping a hand on his knee, and placed the call. After several seconds, she hung up. "Mayfield and Pinson are on a call. I'm going in alone." She held up a hand to stop his protest. "No, it will be fine. No one is here anymore, Everis. I'll be back in thirty minutes." She gave him a quick kiss and disappeared through the fireplace, leaving him feeling like a total failure.

Ten minutes later, he forced himself back inside. Using the pin light on his keychain, he raced through the tunnels. If he hurried, if he couldn't see the walls closing in on him, maybe he could make it.

He caught sight of Shar's flashlight beam and increased his pace.

She whirled, gun drawn. "Everis Hayes! I could have shot you."

"Sorry. I felt stupid staying back there while you came in here alone."

"Men." She shook her head and continued. They came to a dead-end. "Feel around for a switch or handle of some kind."

He swallowed against the bile rising in his throat and concentrated on his breathing. He hand slid over the walls covered with protruding tree roots. Not helping any to know foliage grew on top of them.

"Got it." Shar shoved her shoulder against the wall and sunlight streamed in.

"Can we walk the long way around?" Everis took a deep breath and stepped into the light.

She grinned. "Yes, we can." She waved her arm. "Think of the history we've uncovered. Bad history, but still worth reporting. This is how those children were moved all those years ago."

"Now, they're transported in plain sight in a vehicle." His heart rate subsided, and his breathing returned to normal. "It's easier now."

She nodded. "It's also easier for us to catch the bad guy. I'm calling in a forensic team to scope the house and tunnel. Even thirty-year-old DNA has been known to solve a crime."

"It sure helped in catching Townsend." Of course, they'd had to take the DNA of just about every man in Highland Springs, but finding out the killer was related to Shar had been the crack that allowed them to catch a killer.

They'd find the ones abducting the children and see they served a lifetime behind bars.

CYNTHIA HICKEY

Chapter Six

That woman was not nice to the children. Amy babysat the boy and baby girl as the other woman worked. As if sitting at a desk all day was work. She locked the poor things in the closet when all they did was act their age. Selling them to only God knows who. It was time to save them.

"Come on, my angels. It's time to go." She could take them to the sheriff's office and drop them off. No one would be the wiser. Yes. That was a good idea. She'd do it while it was still dark outside.

She didn't bother dressing them. Time was of the essence. She had to get out of the house while "that woman" was in the shower. "Quickly now."

They slipped into the dawn, inching the door closed behind them with a soft click. With the baby on her hip and holding tightly to the little boy's hand, she headed toward the sheriff's office. A fifteen-minute walk, no more. "Hurry, Brian. Can you run?"

He nodded and jogged at her side.

Amy glanced over her shoulder. The bathroom light still shone. They would make it.

When they reached the front steps, she sat the

children down. "Stay here, Brian. Watch over the baby. Do not go anywhere. Do you understand?"

He nodded.

"Someone will be along to get you. Stay." She placed a kiss on his forehead, glad to be rid of the evil she'd been involved in. A bus ticket sat in her purse next to an envelope carrying enough money to help her settle somewhere else. She'd be fine.

She practically ran for the bus stop. Freedom awaited.

"Amy." That woman stepped from the shadows. "Where are my children?"

"They aren't yours. They never were." Amy clutched her purse.

"What did you do with them?" She pointed a gun at Amy's head.

"I turned them into the sheriff." Sweat beaded on Amy's brow. "I'm done with this business."

"Yes, you are." She pulled the trigger.

The Child Saver dropped the gun and removed her gloves. Shoving them into her pocket, she darted toward the sheriff's office. Too late. That bimbo in a tight skirt and heels pulled into the drive. She shouldn't have gotten rid of the gun so soon.

The woman's shrill voice grated as she tottered toward the children. *My children.* Gone, snatched, like her daughter all those years ago. No matter. She'd find more. She stepped into the shade of an oak tree as the bimbo carried her babies into the building.

"Say that again." Shar clutched her phone tighter in her fist as Amber rambled on the other end.

"I found them on the steps. Just left there."

"I'm on my way." She hung up and called Everis. "Meet me at the office right now. Someone dropped off a couple of children."

"Race you." Click.

Shar smiled and dashed for her jeep. Seriously? She lived much closer than the motel room he rented. Her hand was on the door handle of the building when Everis roared to a stop. She flashed a grin and stepped inside.

Her knees sagged at the sight of the little ones. "Brian?" She turned when Everis entered. "He's back."

Everis approached the little boy and knelt in front of him. "Hello, Brian. Are you hungry?"

He nodded. "Baby, too."

"Let's take care of that."

The phone rang. Amber answered, then hung up. "There's a body on Main. Shot in the head."

Shar motioned for Everis to stay. "I'll handle this. You see whether this little man can tell you anything."

"Thank you." His eyes shimmered. He scooped Brian into his arms. "Amber, bring the little one into the conference room, please. We'll also need to have her checked out at the hospital and the mother called."

Thank you, God, for bringing home two more. Shar rushed to her jeep, calling for whichever deputy was free to meet her. It happened to be Pinson who was standing over the body when she arrived.

He'd strung crime scene tape and kept the media back, but cameras flashed, and microphones were thrust toward Shar when she exited her vehicle. "Come on, folks. I just got here. I don't know a thing." Shaking her head, she ducked under the tape.

47

"The shooter dropped the weapon after killing the victim. Do you know her?"

Shar stared down at the petite Hispanic woman. "Never seen her before." She glanced back to the office, then down again at the woman. "Two of the missing children showed up on the steps of the office today. Maybe she's the one who brought them."

"A partner killed her?"

"Maybe." Shar knelt close to the body. "Have you checked for identification."

He handed her a plastic bag with a driver's license inside. "Amelia Rodriguez. Missouri license. You might be onto something, Sheriff."

"Hmm." Shar slipped on a pair of rubber gloves and opened the victim's purse. An empty envelope, a pacifier, lipstick—definitely a woman who had at least something to do with children. "Get her prints. Once the medical examiner is finished here, come back to the office. This poor woman is our first solid lead."

Shar waved off the reporters and climbed into the safety of her jeep. She stared up and down the street before leaving. The victim didn't appear to have driven a vehicle. There had been no keys in her purse. If she was the one who'd dropped off the children, she had to live close by. A one-year-old could grow heavy mighty fast, not to mention the difficulty a toddler would have in keeping up with the pace of an adult.

Instead of heading back to the office, she circled the reporters and cruised slowly through town. One street to the north had a few homes. One street the other way, a few more. There was a fairly new housing development not much further, but she couldn't see Brian walking that far or the tiny woman carrying a baby that distance. They'd have to go door to door.

She circled and headed back to the office. Once there, she followed the sound of a crying woman.

"Ma'am, she had to go to the hospital to be checked out." Everis shook his head, one hand on Brian's shoulder, whose bottom lip quivered. "You're free to go with her."

"I ain't got insurance."

"That's fine," Shar said. "We'll have you taken to the clinic. Your baby looks well taken care of. This is only a precaution. Please, have a seat and I'll get you a cup of coffee." She glanced at Everis whose face was drained of color.

The day was filled with too much emotion. Shar's hand shook as she poured coffee into a plain white mug. By the time she returned to the conference room, an ambulance arrived to take the baby and her mother to a doctor.

Shar sat in one of the conference chairs, mug in hand, and propped her feet on the tabletop. She studied Everis and the little boy over the rim of her cup. The child had to be Everis's son. The resemblance was remarkable. "Did you take DNA samples of Brian?"

"Yeah. I swabbed his mouth. It doesn't matter, though. He's mine."

Shar's heart gave a lurch. She'd really wanted to be the child's mother. "Once Mayfield gets here, I'm pounding the pavement. Whoever kept these two couldn't have lived far. I believe the victim may be the one who turned the children in. She couldn't have walked far."

"I'd like to come with you."

"Let's get Brian checked out by a doctor. Candy's

off today. She'll watch him, and he can keep Goliath company."

Brian was declared healthy, and now Everis experienced the pain of leaving his child with someone else for the first time. How did mothers do this every day? He'd only discovered he had a child, and now wanted to do nothing more than to get to know his son. But duty called, and there were other children to find.

"Come on, Dad." Shar clapped him on the shoulder and laughed. "He'll be here when you get back. No one will bother him with Goliath around."

"That's for sure." Candy grinned down to where Brian was using the dog as a pillow while eating a peanut butter and jelly sandwich. "They'll both need baths, though."

Everis joined in the laughter. "I'm being silly." He turned to Shar. "First, I show my weakness at being afraid of the dark. Now this. I'm a mess."

Shar tapped his nose with her finger. "A loveable mess. I think it's cute. Ready to knock on some doors? Mayfield started with the north side; we get the south."

"You think I'm cute?" He leaned closer, whispering in her ear. He loved the way she trembled when his lips got close. "I'd like to kiss you, but work calls."

"You can kiss me when we find the one responsible for ripping apart families." She stepped back and headed for the door.

He chuckled and jogged after her, taking one last glance over his shoulder at his jelly-faced son. His son. Would he ever get used to saying those words?

By the time they'd knocked on their third house and interrupted their third housewife from her soap opera, sweat poured down Everis's back. The mid-summer day was brutal. At the next house, Shar cupped her hands around her eyes and peered through a slit in the curtains.

"No one home?" he asked.

"Doesn't look like it." She stepped back and studied the house. "This is a rental with a fairly consistent turnaround of residents. The last woman who lived here was eighty and didn't have children. There's a walker inside and toys on the floor."

"Who's the landlord?" Everis tried the door handle. Locked.

"A management company. I'm calling them now." She pressed buttons on her phone, gave the address, and listened.

Everis strolled around the perimeter of the home, pushing open the gate to a six-foot wooden fence. A well-kept yard, clean windows, a private backyard. Didn't look like a place where children lived. At least on the outside. Where were the yard toys?

"Our friendly neighborhood librarian lives here," Shar said, joining him. "Want to go pay her a visit?"

"Not especially. That woman gives me the creeps."

"Chicken."

"Not everyone can slip on a mask and look as tough and removed as you. You've a special skill."

"It's tough being a woman sheriff." She pulled the gate closed behind them, and they exited the backyard. "I can't go around with smiles all the time. No one will take me seriously."

If she only knew how beautiful she was when she put on her sheriff mask. Blue eyes that hardened to sapphires, raven-black hair pulled away from a face

CYNTHIA HICKEY

with no imperfections other than a tiny scar next to her right eye. He ran his finger down it. "How did you get this?"

"Jumping on the bed. I fell off and bumped my head. Scared the pee-diddle out of Candy. Head wounds bleed a lot."

"The scar keeps you from being perfect." His gaze settled on her full lips.

"I'm far from perfect. My legs carry more scars from bicycle wrecks than should be allowed by law."

"Can I see them?"

She frowned. "I've worn shorts plenty of times."

"I'd like to study them in depth, with my hands."

"Oh, hush. We're working, not flirting." She headed for the jeep.

"Can't I do both?" Everis moved to follow and caught sight of a gray van parked two doors down. "Shar, the van."

She whirled."

With a screech of tires, the van sped away.

Shar and Everis flung themselves into the jeep and gave chase.

Chapter Seven

"**They saw me.**" The Child Saver pounded the steering wheel and ignored the cries of the two small children in the back. "Shut up! You're buckled in. No need to be afraid." She'd gone to the playground to soothe the ache of losing Devin and Darcy and couldn't help but take these two. Their nanny, babysitter— whatever she was—had been too busy texting to notice her charges being lured away. Stupid!

She glanced in the rearview mirror. Now, the sheriff and her sidekick bore down on her. What a day. She needed a hot bath and a glass of wine. She'd had to shoot Amy. Nothing else she could do. Now she'd taken two more children and had no one to help her care for them or post their pictures on the website.

She cursed and whipped the wheel to the right. She'd have to do everything herself. Life was so unfair. "I said to zip it! I can't concentrate on my driving. If we get into a car wreck and burst into a ball of flames, you'll be sorry."

"Great. A roadblock." As if that would stop her. She veered right again, rocketing across a dirt lot and onto a different road. The jeep followed.

If she didn't lose them, she wouldn't be able to go back to work. It was only a matter of time before they discovered that Rachel Smith, aka Dorothy Mansfield, were one and the same. She'd have to leave town. The bank had enough of her money. She could head to Canada and live like a queen.

The van hit a pothole and the children shrieked. "Just tune them out, Rachel. You can do this. Mother would be so proud of your accomplishments." She yanked the wheel left. "I need to ditch this van and you children. Take off on my own. I'll wait it out for a few days, then get what's mine and leave this horrible excuse for a town."

She drove through the barricade to a car wash. Just as the water started spraying, she exited the van, a little water never hurt anyone, and ran. She was quite fast for a fifty-five-year-old. By the time the van made it through the wash, she'd be back home and in dry clothes.

"This person is a psycho." Shar stopped as the van burst into a closed car wash. The water started automatically. "Tell that idiot in the booth to shut it down." She laid on the horn.

The young man shuffled toward them. "You can't go in until the cycle is finished. Then, arrest that person for going in before I was ready."

"I'm going to arrest you if you don't shut it down." Shar glared. "Now."

"Okay." He scowled and hit a switch on the wall.

Before the water had completely stopped, Shar and Everis were dashing for the van. The screams of children came from inside. Shar drew her weapon and jumped next to the driver's side door. Everis did the same on the other side.

The seat was empty. Further investigation showed the van was empty except for two twin girls around the age of three.

Shar slid open the back door and drew one into her arms as Everis did the same with the other. "At least these are two the kidnappers didn't get. Did you get a glimpse of the driver?"

"Nope." Everis patted the child's back in an attempt to soothe her.

"I did." The attendant chewed on a cuticle. "It was the librarian."

Shar froze. "Are you sure?"

"Positive. I can't ever forget that witch. She banned me from ever checking out another book just because my dog chewed the corner of *Moby Dick*."

Shar thrust the child she held into the attendant's arms and called Mayfield. "I'm texting you an address. It belongs to Dorothy Mansfield. Arrest her." She took the child back and moved to the jeep.

"I called Child Protective Services," Everis said, setting the child on the hood. "They'll be here soon."

Shar's phone vibrated. "Sheriff."

"Got a frantic babysitter here that says twin girls were stolen from the park." Amber smacked her gum. "What do you want me to do with her?"

"Tell her to wait. We're on our way." She hung up and glanced at Everis. "Cancel CPS. The person responsible for these darlings is at the office."

Shar had a few choice words to say when they arrived. How could someone take their eyes off three-year-olds long enough for them to be snatched? Didn't

55

anyone pay attention to warnings on the news? In the paper?

Everis pulled out the two car seats Shar had purchased a couple of days ago from the back of the jeep while she held onto the now-quiet little twins and secured them in the back seat. Soon, they had arrived at the office and faced a tear-stained, nineteen-year-old nanny.

"We will not release these children into your care." Shar marched past her. "You were negligent in your job. They will only be released into their parents' custody."

"But, they'll fire me."

"You should have thought of that before taking your attention off them." Shar headed for the conference room. "Amber, get some cookies from the vending machine, please."

"Sheriff Camenetti, please. I need this job. I'm saving for college."

Everis stepped in front of the girl to prevent her from following Shar down the hall. "You heard the sheriff. My advice to you is for you to leave before she arrests you for the negligence she accused you of."

Shar grinned. Everis might have his quirks, like being afraid of dark places, but she liked having him on her side.

"I'm going to provide backup to Mayfield," Everis told Shar once the nanny had left. "He doesn't want to approach the house alone."

"Makes sense, since she'd already shot one person today." Shar set the children on the floor and gave them a couple of stress balls to play with.

Everis watched for a moment as she gazed upon them. She'd make a wonderful mother if given the chance. Maybe he could give her that chance.

Mayfield was sitting in his squad car when Everis joined him and leaned through the window. "You going to sit there all day?"

The deputy chuckled. "Are you sure grouchy Mansfield is the one taking the kids?"

"It seems that way." Everis glanced at the house. "Where's Deputy Pinson?"

"Called into the high school. Someone found pot in the boy's bathroom."

With one hand on his gun, Everis and Mayfield approached the house. He rapped sharply three times on the front door, then stepped back. "Sheriff's office."

It didn't surprise him that no one answered. He reared back and kicked in the door.

It wasn't the same neat scene from earlier that morning. It was obvious someone had been there since. In addition to the few toys on the floor, papers were strewn around, a torn duffel bag tossed in the corner, and the back door was wide open.

Everis whirled and glared at Mayfield. "She was here and escaped out the back. Didn't you check the house?"

"No. The sheriff is emphatic that we not approach dangerous situations without backup."

Everis dashed out the back door. A back gate, cleverly disguised to look like part of the fence, hung open. Nothing but trees on the other side for half a mile, then the interstate. Mansfield was most likely gone.

Still, in order to keep from throttling the deputy—he'd let Shar have that pleasure—he scanned the ground for tracks. There. Mansfield had been so confident in her escape she hadn't bothered to hide her prints.

He sprinted along the trail she'd left and stopped at the edge of the interstate as a blue sedan disappeared over the hill. He had no idea if it was her or not, but he'd bet his favorite pair of boots it was. They'd missed her by minutes. He pulled out his radio and put out an APB before rejoining the deputy.

Ignoring the man's long face, Everis told him to secure the scene. Still fuming, he drove back to the office.

"What do you mean she was there but got away?" Shar was alone, the babies having been picked up by two very angry parents.

"Exactly what I said. Your deputy sat in his car while the woman escaped out the back."

"I'm going to tar and feather him." She threw one of the stress balls at the wall.

"I put out an APB, but without a license plate number, I don't hold out much hope." He picked up the other ball and squeezed, imaging it to be Mayfield's neck.

"While you were gone, I checked into Mansfield's past." Shar slid her laptop next to Everis and sat down. "I thought, what if she is the daughter of the woman who lived in that old Victorian." Her eyes sparkled.

"And?" He peered at the screen.

"I found a school photo of Rachel Smith. Looks familiar, doesn't she?"

He stared at the face of a much younger, smiling Dorothy Mansfield. "So, she's carrying on the family tradition."

"If they're related to the Smiths who ran the home, which I'm assuming at this point they are." She opened another browser. "Then, I discovered that Rachel quit school her junior year for mysterious reasons and was later seen with an infant, but no husband. Then, a few months later, no baby. Said baby daddy took her daughter. No one has seen it since."

"Motive."

"Bingo." She held up her hand for a high five.

Everis obliged. "All we have to do now is catch her."

"Don't burst my bubble, Everis."

"I wouldn't dream of it." He leaned back in his chair. "Everything has fallen into place except for her."

"The Smiths were known for taking children out of unworthy homes and adopting them out to better ones." She wiggled her eyebrows. "Also, they took in pregnant teens and adopted out the babies. The teens were paid a good sum of money and sent on their way. What if we set a trap?"

"Like we did with Townsend?"

"Yes. We get an agent to pretend to be pregnant, spread the word she's looking for adoptive parents, and let Smith come to us."

"What if she's finished abducting?" Everis picked up a pencil and tapped the eraser against the table. "If she's been doing this as long as we suspect she has, she's a very rich woman."

Shar shrugged. "I don't think she can quit. I think it's become an addiction. An adrenaline rush."

"It's a gamble."

"One I think we should take. While we're doing that, we search for her daughter. She would be close to my age. No one disappears completely."

"Not completely." But they can be almost impossible to locate. Shar's idea held some merit. They had no other plan, but Smith could be fleeing further and further away. He'd escape if he were her and start somewhere new.

"We need to alert the departments in surrounding states to be on the lookout. I don't think your plan will work, but I'm willing to give it a go." He met her gaze. "I'll phone the department and see who they can send. "

"You found him?"

Everis turned at the sound of Brianna's voice. "Yes."

"May I see him? Only for a minute."

He stood and approached her. The smell of beer emanated from her from three feet away. "You're drunk and not in any shape to spend time with a child. Is that what you did with the money I gave you?"

Shar's head snapped up, and her eyes widened. He'd have to explain it was child support, not a payoff. If you thought about it, he supposed it was a payoff of sorts. He didn't care. This woman needed out of his son's life until she straightened up hers.

"Sheriff, you ready to call it a day?"

She nodded, glancing from him to Brianna. Without a word, she squeezed between them and left the conference room.

"He's my son," Brianna hissed. "I'll take you to court."

"We've already talked about this. You agreed to let me have him. No judge in the world will give him to a drunk and an addict. Watch for custody papers, Bri. They'll be coming." He stepped out and left her alone.

Chapter Eight

Shar moved slowly through Mansfield house, her gaze roaming every surface and bump in the wall. She opened every drawer for secret hiding places. Coming from a family who'd stolen children for decades, there had to be some type of paper trail.

"Shar?"

Everis's voice caught her by surprise. She spun around to face him. "You got Brian settled in okay?"

"Yeah, the day care you recommended seems like a good one. The techs have scoured Mansfield's slash Smith's, laptop and found nothing incriminating. Nothing that points to anything illegal."

"How is that possible?" Shar opened the freezer. A credit card, frozen in a block of ice, sat on top of ice cream. Obviously, the woman watched her charge card limits. "The black market for babies takes place online nowadays. Has anyone located the site?"

He exhaled sharply through his nose. "It's heartbreaking how many sites there are. We're shutting them down, but they'll pop up again. The problem is determining which one is Smith's and who runs the others. It's going to take months to stop this trafficking."

He was right. They'd shut down Smith and others like her, and two more would start up. She removed the credit card and set it on the counter to thaw before heading to the bathroom. Her gaze met Everis's briefly. A flicker of confusion marred his face.

For two days, ever since Brian's mother had caused a scene at the office, Shar had avoided Everis as much as possible. It shouldn't bother her that he had such a past, but to see it every day, to know it would affect their relationship—it did bother her. She needed time to evaluate the situation and figure out where to go from there.

"I wish you'd talk to me." Everis stood in the doorway. "Whatever is bothering you can be worked out."

"Can it?" She lifted the tank lid to the toilet and pulled out a baggie. "Our Miss Smith might be addicted to pain medications. We can check with—"

"Stop it and talk to me." His face reddened. "Is it Brian?"

She sighed. "I just need time to wrap my head around it all." She met his tortured gaze. "It was hard enough when you left to go undercover last year. Now, you're back and I had hope—what happens next, Everis? You have a son. What do you have planned for your future? You can't go deep undercover anymore."

"Let's solve this case, then I'll figure out where to go next."

"I'm not sure I want to wait until you figure it out. My heart can't take it again." She put the baggie into a paper sack and opened a drawer in the vanity. Several medication bottles rolled around. She dropped them into the sack, trying not to dwell on Everis's intense eyes that followed her every move.

"What if my future plans include you?"

She glanced up. "Let me know when you decide."

He reached out and took a hold of her arm as she slid past him. "Don't shut me out. Please."

Her heart ache was physical. A painful throbbing deep inside her. "Let's focus on the job at hand."

"In a minute." He pulled her close. "I'll find a way, Shar."

She smelled the coffee he'd drunk earlier on his breath. Her gaze flicked to his lips. Would it be such a bad thing to take each day as they came? Could she let her emotions loose only to have Everis leave again? She closed her eyes and leaned her forehead against his chest. "We should check her computer at the library."

"You're killing me." He tilted her face to his and placed a gentle kiss on her lips. "Have faith in me."

"I'll try."

They headed back to the jeep where Goliath drooled out the window. Shar patted his head and climbed in. "You're a beast, dog."

"He'd give his life for you." Everis slid into the passenger side.

"I hope he never has to."

The dog stayed in the jeep again at the library, making a small whine deep in his throat. "I'll let you out when we reach the office. Be a good boy and stay." Shar kissed the top of the dog's head and followed Everis into the building.

Rachel cursed. They were going to find stuff she meant to keep hidden. She'd thought working at the library to be a foolproof plan. She'd been wrong on so many counts. Still, life went on and there was money to be made.

She smiled at the infant in the carrier. So easy to pay off some people. Slip a few hundred into the right person's hands, and you could get anything you wanted. If newborns didn't bring in so much cash, she'd keep the little one for herself. Instead, she'd find a way to get Devin back. He was hers, same as Darcy. That sheriff and agent would pay, oh, yes, they would.

Way back in the woods sat a cabin owned by the Smiths once upon a time. She doubted anyone knew about it anymore. With the hotspot on her phone and a new laptop, Rachel could upload the baby's picture to the couple that contacted her a few days ago. Roughing it a bit wouldn't kill her. She wasn't a delicate flower.

She moved the baby from the car to the cabin and set it on a faded plaid sofa. After spreading a white baby afghan, she placed the child just so and snapped its picture. Voila. She hit *send* and sat back to wait. Within the hour, her bank account was a hundred thousand dollars thicker, and she had a meeting place on the Arkansas/Missouri border.

Rubbing her hands together, she laughed. "Oh yes, baby. Here we go." She dug in her purse and pulled out a prescription bottle of Vicadin. Nothing. Empty. She reared her head back and howled.

Wait. She could do this. She'd make the delivery, then find some punk on the street to give her a fix until she could find a doctor to give her a prescription.

After putting the baby in the backseat, she sped toward the meeting place a little over an hour away. She'd approached the couple last year about adopting, but they hadn't been ready. Now, here she was, risking everything for stupid people.

In the parking lot of a Wal-Mart, she made the exchange. "I'm sure you will be a very happy family," Rachel said as the new mother hugged the infant to her chest. "Tell your friends how to contact me. I'm fresh out right now, but soon another mother will want to put her child up. They always do." She pocketed the cash, no checks for her, and drove to the seedy side of St. Louis. Three hours later, high on pain meds, and with a new prescription in her pocket made out to Mary Lou Smith, she headed back to the rickety cabin.

* * *

Everis hung up the phone. "Rachel Smith was spotted in St. Louis. A young man just sold her pills, then left an anonymous tip at the police station."

Shar turned from the computer screen. "She's back in Missouri?"

"At least for a while."

"One thing at a time. Smith really must not have expected to get caught. Her password was selling babies. Look at the hundreds of pictures and birth certificates on this site. Look." She pointed to one. "Devin Smith. How much do you want to bet this is Brian's?"

Everis leaned over her shoulder. "This will help us find the babies she sold. We hunt down these names and do some foot traffic."

"And break some new mamas' hearts." Shar straightened in her chair. "No help for it, though. The babies belong with their birth parents." She loaded up the computer. "Calling everyone is going to be a long job."

"We'd better get started." Everis carried the computer to the jeep. If criminals of this sort kept showing up in Highland Springs, they were going to need another deputy. He smiled as his mind worked on a plan for the future that might, if he were lucky, involve a certain raven-haired beauty.

The aroma of pizza reached them before they entered the conference room. Everis's stomach growled, reminding him he hadn't eaten in four hours.

Goliath bounded ahead of them.

Pinson shouted. "Keep him away."

Shar laughed. "Sit, Goliath." She moved the pizza box to the center of the table. "Don't put it in his reach if you aren't going to share."

"I wasn't expecting him." Pinson frowned. "I like dogs as much as the next guy, but this thing is a brute."

"A gentle giant." She wrapped her arms around the dog's neck, then reached for a slice of pizza. "You can have my crust, boy."

"We've a big job." Everis set the laptop on the table and explained about the birth certificates. "The best way is to make a list and divide the responsibility."

Mayfield cringed. "We're going to make a lot of people unhappy."

"Yes, we are." Everis reached over and snagged a slice. "I'd better order another one."

"I'll get it." Shar placed the call, then tossed her crust to Goliath who caught it midair.

It took the rest of the afternoon to make the list. The amount of birth certificates was astounding. "One hundred and two," Everis said. "This is the worst thing I've ever encountered. How long has she been doing this?"

"My guess is she's been selling babies most of her adult life. Probably since her own child disappeared." Shar handed each of them a sheet of paper. "Start calling. Stop at nine p.m. We're disturbing these people enough as it is. I'm doing my calling from home. Everis, I'll put the coffee on."

"I accept."

"What about us?" Pinson glowered. "I could use some coffee."

Shar laughed. "Come on, then. We'll all drink until we're jittery."

Darn. Everis had hoped to have some private time with Shar even if they were working.

The four sat around Shar's kitchen table while Candy made flirty eyes at Pinson. Between making coffee and whipping up a batch of chocolate-chip cookies, what had started out with an almost party vibe changed dark once they started searching the names on their lists.

Everis located a little girl, now in the first grade, in San Francisco. He cleared his throat and dialed the number.

"Hello?"

"Yes, this is Arkansas Federal Bureau of Investigations Agent Hayes. I'm looking for Mr. and Mrs. Randolph."

"This is Mrs Randolph. Should I sit down?" Her voice caught. "It isn't my husband, is it?"

"No, ma'am, and yes, please sit down."

"Okay. You can tell me now."

Everis closed his eyes and took a deep breath. "Mrs. Randolph, we have reason to believe that your daughter Cheri was adopted via the black market. Would you mind telling me where the adoption took place?"

Silence filled the space for several minutes. "We paid a woman good money for my daughter two years ago. She was orphaned."

"No, ma'am. She was abducted and sold. I'll send local law enforcement to your house to take a DNA test."

"And arrest me? I swear to you I had no idea Cheri was abducted. Please, don't take my baby away." She broke into sobs.

"We have to search for the birth parents, ma'am."

"You'll have to find us first. We have enough money to flee the country. I'm not giving up my child." Click.

Everis sighed and called to place a flight ban on the Randolphs.

Chapter Nine

Shar glanced at the clock on the wall. Nine fifteen. Tearing apart people's lives because of one person's wrongdoing was exhausting. "I don't ever want to do that again."

"I didn't get through my list," Everis said. "I'll be back at it in the morning. The deputies echoed his statement.

"I didn't either." Shar sighed. Most of the women cried, the men cursed, and only two couples agreed to bring back the infants they'd adopted. Most of them had the children for years and considered them theirs in every way that mattered. Never in a million years would she have thought Highland Springs could ever be in the middle of child trafficking. "That's it, boys. Head on home and meet me in the office at nine a.m."

Her cell phone rang. She pulled it from her pocket. The call came from the service they used to forward calls at night. "Sheriff Camenetti." She listened in silence for a few minutes, then hung up and glanced at Everis. "Ready for a domestic disturbance call?"

"Sure. Hopefully, it's an easy one and will release some of the stress of making these calls." He stood and stretched, his muscles straining the shirt he wore.

Maybe someday, life would allow her and Everis to explore whatever was between them without a psycho interfering. As soon as the deputies headed home, Shar and Everis drove toward a middle-class neighborhood on the outskirts of town.

"This is where the Simpsons live," Everis said.

"Same neighborhood, different address." Shar parked in front of a two-story brick home with white pillars out front and stared. Every single light in the house seemed to be on. Loud voices drifted through an open window. "Even those with money don't always get along." She shoved open her door and, side by side with Everis, made her way to the porch.

"Thank God." A handsome man in his thirties opened the front door before they could ring the bell. "My wife is having a breakdown. I don't know what to do."

"Does she need an ambulance?" Shar slid past him into a nicely decorated foyer.

"We just came from the hospital." His face fell. "We were there to have a baby, but he died."

"I'm sorry for your loss." Shar stepped into a living room. "Ma'am?"

"Annie Marks. That's my wife's name."

"Ms. Marks?" Shar sat on the sofa next to the weeping woman. "What can I do to help you?"

"Bring me my son." The woman gripped Shar's hands. "He isn't dead. I know he isn't. Everything was fine. I heard him cry, I held him in my arms, then..." she choked, "they told me he died."

Shar glanced at the husband.

The man shrugged. "The nurse said he died. There's

no reason to think she'd lie about such a horrible thing."

"There is!" Annie bolted to her feet. "A mother knows. I'd feel it here." She thumped her chest. "That evil woman on television has our Danny, I know it. She paid somebody money to help her." Her gaze whipped from one person to the next. "Sheriff, you must believe me."

"Ms. Marks. I promise we will do everything in our power to find out what happened. If your son is gone, I'll make sure the hospital gives you an explanation. If he was taken—"

"He was." She snatched a tissue from a box on the glass coffee table.

"Then, we'll make it our top priority to bring him home to you." Shar sent Everis a pleading look. He was much better at calming, well, anyone, than she was.

He nodded and motioned for her to trade places. While he consoled the woman, Shar approached the husband. "I'd like to take a look around, if that's alright." Her tone didn't leave an option.

The man's eyes widened, but he nodded. "The nursery is upstairs, last door on the right."

Shar wandered through the downstairs first, peeking into a bathroom, den, kitchen and formal dining. Was it possible Smith had taken a child from the hospital? How? Cameras were everywhere. Someone on the inside would have had to help. Of course, it wasn't unheard of for an unfortunate accident to have happened, and the more unscrupulous of the staff cover it up.

She opened the door to the nursery. Beautifully done in blues and greens, an ocean scene with a friendly octopus above the crib, its tentacles opened wide as if offering a hug. A mobile with stuffed ocean creatures hung above the crib. The room was perfect and lay in wait for a baby. No, Shar didn't think the parents harmed their child.

It either died, or someone took it. Those were the only two options that made sense to her. She finished searching the other rooms, then rejoined the others downstairs. "We'll let you know what we find out," she told Mr. Marks. "My advice right now is for you to call a doctor and get a sedative prescribed for your wife. I'm not an expert, but she seems to be escalating."

The woman's cries had increased, and she rocked back and forth, her arms clasped around her middle, despite Everis's hand on her shoulder. She repeatedly chanted, "he's not dead, he's not dead."

＊
＊　＊

"How many?" Rachel gripped the burner phone in her hand. "I haven't visited in a month, and you want to tell me that three infants have died? Their parents are waiting for them." She hung up and flounced back on the sofa, cursing when a spring poked her in the back.

She'd have to risk the trip to the maternity house. Set up under the pretense of being a home for unwed mothers, Rachel had seen the benefit of such a place in providing infants to those who wanted them. After all, what teenage girl made a good mother? Isn't that why Rachel lost her own child all those years ago? Because the father said she'd been too young and unfit?

Her time in Highland Springs was coming to an end. She felt it in her bones. Time to move on and start somewhere new. Without Devin and Darcy? She couldn't. She'd have to lay low, maybe spend a few weeks away overseeing the maternity houses, then return and abduct them when the sheriff's guard was down.

But first, she had a stop to make.

＊
＊　＊

Everis matched Shar's stride into the hospital. They headed straight upstairs to the maternity ward. It came as a bit of a shock to see two Eureka Springs police officers in the nursing station. "Arkansas Federal Bureau of Investigations Agent Hayes." He showed them his badge.

"Are you here because of the missing newborn?" Officer Moore, according to his nametag, glanced at the identification. "We got a call fifteen minutes ago that an infant was missing from the nursery."

"A boy by the name of Marks?"

"Yes." The officer frowned.

"We'll need to question everyone on staff here, especially those on duty when the child was born." Everis turned to the lead nurse. "Make it happen."

"We'd also like to see any video," Shar said, stepping up to the counter.

"Nice work on The Silencer case last year, Sheriff," the officer said. "Made headline news."

Shar chuckled. "There was a time when Highland Springs was never on the news."

While they waited for the staff to arrive, Everis headed to room 104. He stepped into the empty room. A bed, a chair, a closet...nothing to raise an alarm. He studied the dry erase board on the wall. The name had been erased, but he could make out Julie.

"I want to speak to this Julie nurse first," he called into the hall.

"She's a temp," one of the nurse's replied.

"Then call the agency." Time was of the essence, and Everis had no patience for excuses. The child could be in Smith's hands already.

Not three minutes later, a nurse approached, her eyes shimmered with unshed tears. "They don't have a record of a Julie, or a nurse being sent to help us."

Everis gritted his teeth. Someone, whether Rachel or this Julie person, had watched for the perfect opportunity. "Any word on the video?"

"Security is bringing it up now." She turned her head to a man in dark pants, white shirt, with a can of pepper spray clipped to his belt.

"Here is all the video of this floor and downstairs exits from the time the Marks baby was born until ten minutes ago." The man handed a jump drive to Everis.

"Where can we view them?"

"Here." The head nurse motioned them to a desk at one end of the nurses station.

Shar and the officers peered over Everis's shoulders as he inserted the jump drive. He fast- forwarded to the part where a nurse entered the room of Mrs. Marks. It was hard to see her features, but it was clear it wasn't Rachel Smith. Another accomplice?

"How many women are helping her?" he muttered, fast-forwarding to another scene where Nurse Julie entered the nursery. He slowed the film and concentrated.

The woman went from crib to crib until she reached Baby Marks. She put the child to her shoulder, tossed a blanket over him, and strolled out as if going on a jaunt to the store. Everis went from exit to exit until he saw her leave by a door on the south side and get into a pickup truck.

"Can we see the plate?" Shar leaned in closer.

"No." Everis slapped his hand on the desk. "We don't even have a clear view of the woman's face."

"But we do know the child didn't die." Shar straightened. "I'll call the parents."

They were fast losing what tenuous grip they had on the case. Everis's stomach churned, sending acid into his esophagus. How many more families were going to be ripped apart before they stopped Rachel Smith? They needed to find the woman's baby daddy. With any luck, the man might be able to give them insight into Rachel's mind.

* * *

Joyce Larson, aka Julie when the need suited her, put the infant boy into a carrier and headed into the mall's east entrance. Twenty-thousand dollars would solve a lot of her problems. It had been such an easy job to watch the hospital, then stroll in and take the baby right under everyone's nose. Maybe she'd offer her services again.

She set the carrier next to the agreed-upon meeting place, a fountain in the atrium, and settled down to wait. The baby started to fuss, making mewling sounds. Joyce hoped the exchange could be made before he opened his mouth and wailed. It wouldn't do to draw attention to herself.

An envelope appeared over her shoulder. Joyce gripped the wrist of the hand holding it. "I'm available again."

The person yanked free. "I have your number." A hand gripped the handle of the carrier. Footsteps sounded as the person walked away.

Joyce opened the envelope and smiled. Fifty-dollar bills—what a wonderful sight. Now to pay off her credit card and buy herself those boots she wanted.

Humming a tune to a song she didn't know, but had recently heard on the radio, she headed for the shoe store, dropping the envelope into her shoulder bag. Yep, Joyce may well have just changed careers. Who needed to wait tables when this kind of money was to be had? She'd never make this much on tips. Unmarried, with no prospects in the future, Joyce was free to do whatever she wanted. Money would make that even more possible.

She stopped and watched the woman who had taken the baby leave through the front doors of the mall. Easy-peasy.

Chapter Ten

"Look at the little darlings." Rachel slowed the car. The baby in the backseat didn't answer, but she knew he heard her. "Would you like some company? They're a bit older than I usually take, but I've been getting orders for older children."

She watched as the boy, maybe eight-years-old, held the hand of a little girl around six. Red hair, a smattering of freckles—they were perfect. She sped up and stopped at the curb ahead before exiting the car. Her heart raced as the children approached.

"Could you help me?" She opened the car door and pointed to the baby. "My son misses his brother and sister. You see, they're with their grandmother, and I thought if you could smile and wave at him, he might be happy. I'll give you five dollars."

The children stopped and stared. "We aren't supposed to talk to strangers," the boy said.

"My name is Rachel. Now we aren't strangers. The baby is Billy." She kept a smile plastered on her face. Hurry up, brat, before someone takes notice.

"We have to get home. Mama doesn't like it when we're late."

"Why are you walking home alone?" Some mother, leaving her children alone to be preyed upon. It would be merciful to take them.

"She works. Daddy went to heaven." He squared his shoulders. "We'll be going now. Bye."

Rachel reached for his arm.

The girl opened her mouth and screamed.

Without a second thought, Rachel slammed the car door, raced to the driver side, and roared away. That was a close one. Those two had been taught a valuable lesson. Probably by their father.

Rachel slowed as she passed the school. Full of children and no one to take. She couldn't lift them over the five-foot fence. She was strong, but not that strong. There had to be a better place. She'd thought of the mall, but cameras were everywhere. Still, she had noticed a door at the end of a hall. Perhaps she should take a closer look when she returned from the maternity house.

Two hours away, nestled in a meadow, stood a white two-story plantation style house that Rachel had purchased for next to nothing and renovated. It was perfect for young women who needed to "get away" for five to six months.

She carried the baby into the house, handed it to a worker with the orders to find a wet nurse, then went in search of the director. She found her in the room designated as her office, a glass in hand that Rachel doubted contained water.

Rachel sat in the chair across from her. "Explain the infant deaths."

Swirling the ice in her glass with a forefinger, the woman who could stand to lose seventy pounds, shrugged. "You don't like us to call for medical attention. Some newborns need a doctor."

"Then get them one."

"That costs more money than you allow me to spend."

Rachel planted her hands flat on the desk and leaned across it until her face was inches from the director's. "Stop the deaths, or I find someone to take your place."

The woman smirked. "Who in the world would take this job for fifty-thousand a year?"

"Plus room and board."

"Whatever." She downed what was in her glass. "I'm surrounded by incompetence, unmarried mothers, and wailing infants. Good luck replacing me."

"Don't press the issue. How many are dead?"

"Twelve at last count. We buried them out back. Do you want to see the graves?"

"Yes." She wouldn't put it past the woman to sell the babies herself. "I'd also like to speak with the mothers. I don't want to have to come back here."

"Most of them have left. There's no reason to stay after the baby is born." The director led Rachel to a plot of land outside dotted with tiny crosses. A million dollars lay buried in the dirt.

* * *

"Brian, would you get my shoes from the closet?" Shar smiled down at the little boy who helped stir the cookie batter. "I need to get these in the oven before we go to the lake with your daddy."

"No."

Shar's eyes widened as she met Everis's gaze over the boy's head. "No?"

"No closet. Mean mama put us in the closet." He continued to stir without lifting his head.

Shar bit her lip to keep from saying something little ears shouldn't be subjected to. From the look on Everis's face, he struggled with the same thing.

"Did the mean mommy hit you?" Everis forced out.

"Sometimes." Brian lifted the stirring spoon to his mouth. "If I didn't eat all my food. She yelled at the baby a lot and made it cry."

"Come here, son." Everis motioned for Brian to sit on his lap. "I think your dad needs a hug."

Shar did, too, but the sight of dark head bent over dark head while little arms wound around Everis's neck was almost just as good. Poor baby. First Brian had known neglect, then abuse and fear. She had no doubt that Everis would do everything in his power to make it up to his son.

Everis's phone lit up on the table. He glanced at the screen and frowned. "We'll have to postpone the lake. Agent Sharp is arriving in thirty minutes."

"Bummer." Shar slid the cookies into the oven. "We'll take Brian and Goliath to the office with us. They can keep each other company." She hadn't wanted to take a day off from finding Rachel Smith, but a little boy needed their attention and his father had little experience with children. Shar would do what she could to help.

The minute the cookies came out of the oven, Shar put them into a Tupperware container, and they all trooped to the jeep. After stationing Brian and the dog behind Amber's desk, she and Everis headed for the conference room.

"This has to be the most unconventional law

enforcement office I've ever been in," Everis said with a laugh. "Kids, dogs, a receptionist with cleavage. Very unprofessional."

"I wouldn't have it any other way." Shar grinned and pushed the conference door open with her hip.

A woman who didn't look more than sixteen sat opposite the two deputies. Despite her youthful appearance, a hard glint shone from the officer's eyes. She stood and held out her hand when Shar and Everis entered. "Detective Sharp. Don't let my looks fool you."

Shar raised her eyebrows. "I wouldn't dream of it. Cookie?" She held out the container.

The deputies didn't need to be asked twice, but Detective Sharp declined, instead focusing a hard stare on Shar and Everis. "We've reason to believe Smith has several homes for unwed mothers scattered around the state." She slid a file across the table. "I plan on finding one and admitting myself."

Shar frowned. "Are you really pregnant?"

"No, it's a prosthetic, but no one needs to know that."

Everis snagged a cookie. "We use Sharp whenever we need someone to go undercover who can pass for high school or college age. Believe it or not, she's thirty."

"How did you find out about the homes?" Shar settled back in her chair.

"It wasn't easy. The woman has more aliases than anyone I've heard of." Sharp folded her hands on the table. "Missouri had a young girl come forward saying she went to a home to have her baby to prevent embarrassment to her family. Only her baby died. She never saw it or held it. Suspecting foul play, she went to the authorities who opened an investigation." She slid across a photograph. "Missouri Maternity Home. 'Where mothers are treated like royalty.'" She shook her head.

The woman seemed to have multiple clones. At least multiple partners in her crimes. The credit card Shar had found in her freezer had a zero balance. She apparently had all the funds she needed. "Arkansas has five such homes. How did the calling to the adoptive parents go?" She transferred her attention to the deputies.

"Not good." Pinson sighed. "Heartbreaking. Only one couple was relieved, and only because the child they adopted turned out to be mentally challenged. They're hiring someone to take it back to Missouri."

"Any more making threats to run?"

"No."

"We'll follow up, but let's close that chapter for now." Shar turned to Everis. "Maybe we could get someone to go undercover as a director of one of these homes."

"Not you. You're too recognizable."

"Not with a wig and contacts." Blue eyes were easy enough to hide and a wig would take care of the hair. "I have a fat suit I wore one year for Halloween. Not even my mother would recognize me. The question now is, how do we get Sharp and me assigned to the right house?"

"Let's go with our gut." Everis grabbed another cookie, then glanced out the door to where Brian raced up and down the hall while Goliath lumbered at his side. He relaxed. No one would bother his son while the dog stood guard. "We visit all five houses and see which one we can infiltrate."

"I know for a fact that Hope for Women is a reputable home," Sharp said. "My sister used them a couple of years ago. I have a gorgeous nephew."

"That leaves four." Shar glanced through the folder. "I'll call and see which ones are associated with a church. It's the one that stands alone and is privately run that we need to focus on." She headed for her office.

The deputies left to answer a disturbance call at a bar by the interstate, leaving Everis alone with Rebecca Sharp, ex-girlfriend. But, high school was a long time ago, and they'd both done a lot of living since then.

Becky wore a secretive smile. "You like her. Not that I blame you. She looks like she belongs on the cover of a magazine wearing nothing more than a bikini. I'd pictured her as a manly type of woman."

"She's nothing like that." Everis took a deep breath. "How have you been?"

"Good. I'm engaged."

"That's wonderful, Becky."

She motioned her head toward the door. "The boy looks just like you."

"I recently found out I have a son. Talk about a shock."

"That's a story I look forward to hearing. Now, about the pretty sheriff." She winked.

He grinned. "Yeah, I like Shar. More than like, if I'm honest with myself. I think she returns the feeling, but until I know what the future holds, we skirt around any serious relationship."

"That's sad. In our line of work, we don't know what the future holds. If you want something, you grab and hold on for however long you can. I plan on getting married and having a baby or two while I can." Becky pushed to her feet.

"You look good pregnant."

"You mean I look like a pregnant teen."

"Yeah, but that's what we need right now." He laughed. "Let me introduce you to my son, Brian."

Shar stood in the doorway of her office, laughing, at Brian who tried to ride Goliath, but the dog kept sidestepping out from under him. At one point, Brian belly flopped across the dog and landed in a heap on the other side.

"Brian, come meet a friend of mine." He held out his hand. "This is someone I knew when I was in school. This is Detective Sharp."

"School?" Shar lifted a brow.

"High School." He almost filled in the questions he saw flickering in her eyes, but then relished the bit of jealousy he read in them. He'd tell her later. Unless she asked. He kind of hoped she cared enough to ask.

Chapter Eleven

"Got it." Shar waved a sheet of paper, hope flickering to life in her chest. "There's a Happiness House in Missouri, Arkansas, Georgia, Alabama, and the Carolinas. None are affiliated with any organization that I can tell."

"Rachel Smith is a busy woman." Sharp shook her head. "When are we paying this place a visit?"

"I think you should go as soon as possible to check yourself in. Scope the place out and see whether or not I can get in as an administrator. If not, we'll come up with another plan."

"Why not bluster your way in?" Pinson cleaned under his nails with a pocketknife. "I know the world is full of unscrupulous people, but there's a chance the current administrator doesn't know we're looking for her boss."

Shar met Everis's gaze. "Would it work?"

"Maybe." He grinned, sending her stomach somersaulting. "I'd feel better about things if you and Sharp were together."

What's the worst that could happen? The current administrator called Shar's bluff and kicked her off the property? She seriously doubted the woman would try calling the authorities. "What are you men going to do while we're gone?"

"Same thing we're doing now. Work at stopping Rachel Smith." Everis stood. "Let's get this phase of taking down a pyscho underway. You'll both need burner phones and aliases with papers. I have a contact that can get these done quickly. Sharp, why don't you plan on heading up there tomorrow and the sheriff the day after?"

"Sounds good." Sharp grabbed her prosthetic belly and put it on under her shirt. "I'd better go fill a backpack with essentials. See you later." She blew Everis a kiss, then exaggerated her waddle out the door.

Shar narrowed her eyes. Don't be ridiculous. Everis has never mentioned a woman in his life, at least not currently.

"Heads up." Mayfield turned from the computer he'd been engrossed in. "Found the man who may, or may not, be Smith's baby daddy."

"Where?" Shar rushed to his side. "How do you know?"

"Mark Lincoln, high school quarterback in the day, straight A student, now teaches PE in Little Rock." He shook his head. "Seems like the guy would have moved farther away, doesn't it? Wait, wait…Bingo! He lives in Eureka Springs now. Moved there last year…still teaches." Mayfield sat back, a grin splitting his face. "Am I good or what?"

"You're awesome." Shar clapped him on the shoulder. "Road trip, Everis?"

"Ready and willing. Lead the way, boss lady." He flashed another killer grin.

Sometimes Shar felt as silly as a teenager when Everis was around. Today was obviously such a day. First jealousy, now she flushed at his grin. Someone needed to knock her over the head.

"So," she said, climbing into the jeep, "just how close are you and Detective Sharp?" She closed her eyes and winced. She'd told herself she wouldn't ask. Here she was asking.

A dimple winked in his right cheek as he shifted in his seat. "You do care."

"About what?" She drove to the interstate.

"Me having someone else."

"Don't be ridiculous." She couldn't stop a smile from spreading. "I'm being silly, I know. We don't have a commitment. You're just someone I enjoy spending time with, and kissing. The kisses are good."

He laughed out loud until tears poured down his face. Once he caught his breath, mere seconds before Shar wanted to throat punch him, he said, "just good?"

"For crying out loud." She increased their speed. The day couldn't be over fast enough for her.

* * *

Rachel's cell phone rang. She pressed the button on her steering wheel that enabled her to speak via blue tooth. "Why are you contacting me?"

"I'm at the mall," Joyce said, "and I have my eye on the cutest toddler. Blond curls, blue eyes…want her? Her mother is preoccupied with shopping. It would be a cinch."

She thought for a moment. It would keep Rachel a bit out of the spotlight to have someone else do the snatching. Yes, yes, she'd said she was going to quit, but whenever she got close, she had to go again. Taking and selling the children, saving them from incompetent parents, had become like a drug to her. Maybe a partner wasn't such a bad idea.

"Alright. Call me when the deed is done, and we'll set up a place to make the exchange." It was a good thing Rachel had a suitcase full of money back at the cabin, and a couple of envelopes full in the glove compartment. Most of her payments went to an offshore account, but paying trolls like Joyce took cash.

Grinning, she sped to her humble home, free of worry and babies for an hour or so. Perhaps she should have Joyce bring the child straight to her? No, best they kept things as anonymous as possible. No one could be fully trusted nowadays. Joyce could turn in an instant, just like Amy.

Rachel's smile faded. She'd thought Amy was her friend. Perhaps the successful and rich couldn't have true friends. Maybe jealousy got in the way. That had to be it. Amy had grown jealous that Rachel made the most money, and Amy was just a glorified babysitter.

Still, murder wasn't usually something Rachel enjoyed doing. Unless someone betrayed her. Then she meted out justice like candy on Halloween.

Her phone rang again. "Got the child. I'm moving quickly through the mall and out a side door before the alarm is sounded. Where do I bring it?"

Rachel had looked forward to a cup of coffee. "Highland Springs Lake, north side parking lot. I'll find you. Sit on the bench facing the lake, the child next to you. Do not turn around, same as before."

Rachel parked and hunkered down in her car as a burgundy Corolla pulled into the lot and parked at the far end away from other cars. Smart girl. Once Joyce was sitting with the curly-haired tot next to her, Rachel grabbed an envelope from the glove compartment and made haste to the bench.

The child glanced up at her, looking so much like the first Darcy, the one the man Rachel had loved stole, that Rachel actually gasped. Joyce started to turn at the sound and got an elbow to the head. "I said not to look back."

Rachel grabbed the child and darted for her car. "I have my girl back." Joy bubbled into laughter. "After all this time, you're home with Mommy." She clipped the little girl into a car seat and climbed behind the wheel.

She glanced to where Joyce stood staring next to her car. Couldn't she follow a simple order? Rachel backed out of the spot and turned the car to face the other woman. When Joyce started toward her, Rachel stepped on the gas.

Joyce couldn't move fast enough. She bounced off the hood and slid like a rag doll to the blacktop.

Darcy wailed from the backseat.

"Don't cry, darling. Mommy had to run her over. We can't take any chances of someone taking you again. All we need to do now is get your brother back. Oh, he isn't your real brother, but we'll love him all the same."

* * *

Everis and Shar waited in the parking lot of the school until Mark Lincoln strolled through the double doors when the bell rang. His brow furrowed when he spotted them, but he continued to approach.

"May I help you?" His gaze flicked to Shar. "Sheriff."

"We would like to ask you some questions about Rachel Smith." Everis showed his badge. "Is there somewhere private we can talk?"

The man paled. "I didn't think I'd ever hear that name again. I don't live far from here, and my wife won't be home for another two hours. You're free to follow." He slid into his car, glanced in his rearview mirror, and drove away with them on his tail.

"He didn't seem as surprised as I thought he would be," Shar said, pulling into the man's driveway behind him.

"I agree. He's been watching the news."

"And didn't come forward with information. Shame on him." Shar pushed open her door and climbed out, Everis doing the same.

Lincoln waited on the porch and invited them inside. "I usually have a beer before I start grading papers. Do you mind?"

"Not a problem." Everis took a seat on the sofa while Shar stood at the fireplace and studied photographs on the mantle as Lincoln left the room. "Do you want to take the lead in questioning?"

"No." She lifted a picture. "You go ahead. Cute girl."

"Despite her mother," Lincoln said, returning with a beer. He sat in a recliner across from them.

"You aren't thrown off balance by our coming." Everis speared the man with what he called his "cop" stare. Unblinking and piercing.

"I saw the press conference." He took a big gulp of his drink. "Back in high school, my fellow football players dared me to." He rolled his head on his shoulders, "I hate admitting I was that cruel. Anyway, they dared me to get Rachel Smith in the backseat of my car. I did. She got pregnant. The quiet shy girl I'd taken advantage of became insane. There was no other word for it."

He finished off the beer and set it on a side table. "Now, as a senior in high school, I had no intentions of being a daddy, but I always took responsibility for my actions."

"That was manly of you." Everis frowned. Was this guy for real? He wouldn't get an honorable ribbon for his actions.

"I know. I was a jerk. Anyway, I realized I didn't want my child raised by a family with rumors floating around that they sold babies. What if Darcy disappeared? So, I took her instead." He smiled at the mantle. "Best thing I ever did. Smart as a whip, and while she might not be the most beautiful woman, she's kind and respectable."

"Any idea where we can find Rachel Smith?"

"No. I haven't kept up with her." He picked at a thread on his pants. "The rumors are true, aren't they? Rachel is stealing and selling children as her parents supposedly did."

"It appears so. It's a generational thing." Everis stood and pulled a business card from his pocket. "We won't take up anymore of your time, but please, if you remember anything at all that will help us catch her, call me."

Lincoln nodded. "Is it possible to keep this from Darcy?"

"We'll do our best, sir, but my advice is for you to come clean. You wouldn't want your daughter to find this out any other way." Everis followed Shar from the house.

"What a dirt bag." Shar marched to the jeep. "Teenagers can be so cruel. Especially jocks." She yanked open the driver side door and got in.

"That sounds like the voice of experience," he said, climbing in on his side.

"Many a boy wanted to get me in the back seat. They seemed to think I was as wild as my parents." She glared at the house. "I wasn't anything like them."

"I never thought you were." He held up his hands as if to give.

"I'm sorry. I get touchy when I run across people like him." She backed from the driveway and headed toward Highland Springs.

Everis's phone rang. "Agent Hayes."

"Pinson here. We have witnesses at the lake that say a woman matching Rachel Smith's description took a kid from another woman, then ran over the other woman. I'm headed there now."

"We'll meet you. Secure the scene and the witnesses." Everis hung up. "Make haste to the north side of the lake. We've a body and an eyewitness."

By the time they arrived, quite a crowd had gathered on the other side of the crime scene tape, and local media had set up shop. Vultures. Everis ducked under the tape and headed for the witnesses, a young couple with fishing gear.

"I'm Agent Hayes. Could you tell me what you saw?"

The woman glanced at the man, then nodded. "We were headed back with our catch when we saw a woman and a little girl sit on that bench over there. I commented on how cute the child was. Then that woman we saw on the news walked up behind them and snatched the child. Then, when the woman who was sitting started walking toward the other woman's car, she ran over her."

"Don't forget that she hit the one woman in the head, dear," the man pointed out. "Although it could have been an accident."

Everis glanced from the woman to the man. "Did the woman on the bench cry out?"

"No. The other woman handed her an envelope."

"It's on the trunk of the Corolla," Pinson said. "Full of cash. I think the victim might have been in cahoots with Smith."

Everis agreed. How many more were out there helping Smith wreck lives?

Chapter Twelve

Rebecca Sharp, aka Lucy Barnes, walked up the brick pathway in the middle of nowhere to sign herself in at Happiness House. She stopped in front of the large double doors. Impressive. The former plantation-style house had been well taken care of.

Muted voices drifted around the corner, luring Becky to investigate. Hitching the backpack more firmly on her back, she stepped around and found herself blocked by a high hedge. "Hello?"

"Shh," someone hissed. "You have to talk softly around here, or Mrs. Stuart gets mad. Go ring the bell."

Shrugging, Becky did as she was told. It took several minutes before a large woman opened the door. Beady eyes peered out of a pudgy face, reddened from too much alcohol.

"Another one. Come on in. Welcome to Happiness House, and good luck. Sign in there, then follow me."

Easy enough. Becky had feared she'd have to be examined by a doctor. No matter how good of a detective she was would she be able to pull that one off. She signed her alias in a large leather book, then followed the woman—she presumed Mrs. Stuart—up a flight of stairs.

At the top, the woman stopped to catch her breath, her chest wheezing. "You're…lucky. We have a bed. Some…days, we're full of little harlots like you." She opened the door to a room that held three twin-sized beds, three small dressers, and two chairs.

A girl who couldn't be more than fifteen, glanced up from a chair in the corner of the room. Her face held a look of pity. "You can have the bed closest to the door." She glanced back at her book.

"I'm Mrs. Stuart. Bathroom is at the end of the hall. Rules are posted on the wall next to the door." She left, closing the door behind her.

"You're older than most of us here," the girl said.

"I'm a senior. Name's Lucy."

"Aggie." She closed her book. "Try to avoid Moose as much as possible. Be invisible, and pray your baby doesn't die. Most of them do. The only room for privacy is the bathroom, but if you're in there more than fifteen minutes, Mrs. Stuart, aka Moose, will unlock the door and force it open. Best she not have to do that." Rubbing her well-rounded stomach, Aggie left Becky alone.

She pulled a cell phone from her pack and sent a quick text that she was there and to check out infant mortality at the house. When she'd finished, she erased the text and stashed the phone back in her pack.

The next morning, Shar stood in the same spot Becky had the day before and took a deep breath. Knowing the current administrator was prone to drink, as Becky's last text of the night stated, Shar's bluff would be easier to pull off.

She rang the bell three times and stepped back, squaring her shoulders. The woman she presumed to be Mrs. Stuart opened the door, her gaze raking over Shar.

"What do you want?"

"Mrs. Stuart?"

"Yeah."

"I'm Ann Link, the new director. You're dismissed, effective immediately. Please pack your personal belongings." Shar met the woman's glare.

"Who said?"

"Mrs. Smith." Shar slipped her mask into place and glanced at her watch. "You have thirty minutes to vacate the property."

"It'll take that long for a taxi."

"Then I suggest you call one before you pack." Shar squeezed past her, catching a glimpse of several wide-eyed mothers-to-be watching from the dining room.

Mrs. Stuart muttered some very unflattering words about Mrs. Smith and lumbered past the stairs to a room at the end of the foyer. Banging quickly ensued, along with a few choice words, before the woman entered again, battered suitcase in hand. "Good luck, Barbie Doll. It's an ungrateful job." She padded outside, slamming the door behind her.

Shar motioned to Becky. "What's your name?"

"Lucy."

"How many girls are here?"

"Fifteen, counting me. I can show you to your office."

"In a minute." Clasping her hands in front of her, Shar surveyed the silent group. "Give me a day to acquaint myself, evaluate the way things were run, then we'll have a meeting to discuss the changes. Any questions?" She smiled.

Expressions of shock flitted across their faces, tugging at Shar's heart. She motioned her head to Becky and let herself be shown to her room.

"Close the door," she said once they were inside. "This looks like a prison." A full-sized bed with a plain blue blanket, a table and chair, one small dresser.

"You have your own bathroom to the left and your office is to the right. Mrs. Stuart enforced rules with an iron fist, literally." Becky plopped onto the chair. "I wish I could get this belly off for five minutes."

Shar laughed. "Do you shower in it?"

"No. That's the only time I can take it off. I make use of every minute of my fifteen allowed." She handed a sheet of paper to Shar. "The rules. It didn't take me but ten minutes to learn Mrs. Stuart spent her life ripped. She's a mean drunk, too. Hates the girls."

"Then, it's a good thing she's no longer here. Were you able to find out the last time Smith visited?"

"It's written on the desk calendar. Just a couple of days ago, to be exact. I tried to get into the filing cabinet after the woman passed out last night, but it's locked up tight. Hopefully, she left you the key."

Shar sat on the bed. "What about the infant deaths?"

Becky swallowed hard. "Just about every single one that is born here dies. The only ones who don't are the ones born to little rich girls whose parents want them out of sight for a while and pay a pretty penny for it." She pushed to her feet. "The others will grow suspicious if I'm in here much longer. We'll talk later." She left Shar alone.

Shar quickly unpacked, then moved next door to her office. After thirty minutes, it became quite obvious she didn't have the key to the cabinet. Darn. She should have asked for all keys from Mrs. Stuart.

She stepped into the hall. "I may be profiling here, but do any of you know how to pick a lock?"

A skinny girl who looked as if she should eat six meals a day raised her hand. "Unless you're going to hit me, then no. But Lucy said you were nicer than the other lady."

"Much nicer." Shar smiled. "Come help me out and you can have an extra slice of cake for dessert. Somebody go make a cake." She waved her arm for the girl to enter. "Or tell the cook to bake one. As long as we have cake, I'll be happy."

* * *

"How's the new home?" Everis asked Shar as he lay in bed, his sleeping son curled up next to him.

"The girls are pretty great, actually. We missed Smith by two days, but according to the residents, she was in and out within half an hour. That's the first time any of them have seen her, and one girl has been here five months."

"So she left the administrator to run things."

"Apparently they mostly communicated via phone. Everis, the filing cabinet is full of falsified birth certificates. This is so much bigger than we thought."

Everis hugged Brian closer. "How big?"

"Hundreds over the course of the last ten years."

His heart froze. The families this woman and her parents had affected. The damage would continue for years to come, even after the children were reunited with their birth parents. How could they stop something that had been going on for over fifty years?

"Missouri is now involved, and I've alerted the

other states where Happiness Homes are located. We'll have the houses closed down within a week."

"Where will the girls go, Everis? Some of them have been kicked out of their homes."

He closed his eyes, his head throbbing from so much distress. "The other houses have promised to make room. They'll be okay, and their babies have a better chance of surviving or being adopted the right way."

"No more sightings of Smith?"

"No, and no more reports of missing children."

"We can't let her disappear."

"We won't." Everis twined his fingers in his son's curls and glanced to where Goliath lay hanging off the end of the bed. "Your dog insists on sleeping in my bed."

She laughed. "He's hard to resist."

"Only because he's too big to fight with. He misses you." *I miss you.*

"I'll be home in a couple of days if things move as fast as you think they will. So much for luring Smith in with a fake pregnant belly."

"We'll catch her some other way. Mayfield is scouring maps and real estate to see whether her family owned any other property."

"Good night, Everis."

"Good night, Shar." He hung up and stared at the ceiling. If Rachel chose to flee the state, change her name and appearance, they might never solve the case, and children would continue to disappear. Failure was not an option. They had to bring her down.

He glanced at sleeping Brian. How must parents who had been with their child since day one function after catastrophe, when he'd almost been destroyed after just meeting his child?

Sighing, he slipped off the bed and padded barefoot to the kitchen. Fixing himself a cup of coffee, he plodded to the window to peer out. Nine p.m. was too early to go to sleep, especially when his mind whirled with what ifs.

A woman stood under the streetlamp across the street. She appeared to be staring at his house. When she turned at a noise down the road, Everis recognized her.

Rachel Smith.

He dropped his mug and shot out the front door.

She squeezed through a hedge and disappeared from sight.

"Oh, no you don't." He darted after her, when she appeared again. "Stop, Rachel Smith!" She glanced over her shoulder and tore off through a back yard of a nearby house.

A dog barked.

Everis turned right.

A sharp pain tore through his foot. He glanced down at a shard of glass protruding from his foot. A broken beer bottle lay nearby. Great. He'd come face-to-face with evil, and she got away again.

He limped back home and straight to the bathroom. When he pulled out the glass, it became apparent he needed stitches.

He glanced at the bedroom. And a babysitter. Not having one, he limped to the bedroom and woke up Brian. "Come on, boy. Daddy has to go to Urgent Care."

"Owie?"

"Yep." He scooped up his son, hobbled to the car and drove off. Mayfield and Pinson were going to have a field day when they found out.

Chapter Thirteen

"I think you can get rid of that belly now." Shar grinned.

"I can put my engagement ring back on." Becky unhooked the prosthetic stomach and pulled a diamond ring from her pocket. "It isn't the same without it on my finger."

"You're engaged?" Relief flooded through Shar as if a dam had burst at the lake. She liked the detective, but that little niggle of jealousy had kept her from fully relaxing.

"Yes." Becky's eyes sparkled. "We're having a Christmas wedding. He's a nice, safe, slightly boring school teacher who cringes every time I go on assignment. Isn't that cute?"

Shar laughed. "Let's go tell the girls who we really are and start these interviews."

Murmurs began the moment they stepped into the dining room at breakfast. Aggie narrowed her eyes. "Did you have your baby last night? Did it die?"

Shrieks filled the room.

Shar raised a hand to halt the noise. "This is Detective Sharp. I'm Sheriff Camenetti. We're investigating the reason behind all the infant deaths. Detective Sharp's pregnancy was part of our undercover. I'd like to question each of you separately after breakfast."

One girl crossed her arms. "What if we refuse?"

"Then, we'll cart you to the police station." Shar smiled. "Any more questions? We'll make the process as painless as possible. Really, we're here to help you and your babies. Nothing more than that." She snagged a biscuit and jam from a plate in the center of the table and headed for the kitchen.

The cook, a quiet woman by the name of Alice, counted cans of soup in the pantry. "We're almost out. Shall I place an order? The other lady wanted me to ask for permission."

"There's no need." Shar took a bite of the biscuit. "I'm Sheriff Camenetti." She removed the blond wig, then the brown contacts.

"I thought you looked familiar." The woman smiled. "I hope you're here to shut this place down."

"Curious statement from someone who lives and works here."

"I need the job. Without me, those girls wouldn't have decent food. Aggie? She's my granddaughter. There's no way in Hades I'd let her mother kick her out of the house and not tag along."

"Sheriff?" Becky stood in the doorway. "We're ready to start."

"I'd like to speak with you more, Alice." Shar turned and ignored the whispers as she marched to her office. Into the kitchen a blond, out with dark hair. The girls would have plenty to talk about while waiting their turn.

Little Miss What-If-We-Refuse entered the office first and took a seat before being told. Black eyes peered from a face the color of creamed coffee. Full lips twisted in scorn. "I know the drill. My name is Mira Engstrom. I'm seventeen-years-old. I'm giving my baby to my sister, if she still wants it, and if it lives."

"Thank you, Mira." Shar took care not to let her mask slip into place. "You seem very familiar with police procedure."

"I've had my share of run-ins. My probation officer sent me here."

"His name?"

"Joe Wick. He's a grumpy old fart."

Shar wrote his name down. A probation officer sending one of his charges to Happiness House would be worth questioning. Too many people seemed to be helping Smith, all for a quick buck. "How much time did you serve?"

"Six months for prostitution. If you're thinking I don't know the baby daddy, you're correct."

It was sad how jaded the seventeen-year-old was. "Have any of you seen a doctor?"

"Nope. That old bat who runs this place didn't care enough."

Shar jotted a note to have them seen as soon as possible. "You mean Ms. Stuart?"

"No, the other one. She doesn't visit often, but I've seen her hanging around."

Shar glanced up from the paper in front of her. "What do you mean?"

Mira shrugged. "She paces the property line at least once a week. Spying is my guess."

"How do you know she's the one in charge?"

"Because Ms. Stuart would go out there to meet her, then complain about strange bosses." Mira stood. "Can I go now? This baby is pressing on my bladder."

Shar chuckled and nodded. While she waited for the next girl, she sent Everis a text to check out Joe Wick and have someone watch the perimeter of the grounds surrounding the house. Mira may not have wanted to talk, but she'd spilled enough information to give Shar and the others a way to move forward on a case threatening to stall.

One by one, the girls trooped in, but none had given Shar as much information as Mira. Maybe there was a way Shar could help the girl as a reward. Help her get on the right path in life.

"Ready for me?" Alice entered the room. "The girls sound like a bunch of chickens out there, sharing what they've told you. Stuart would have had a fit at the racket. It's music to my ears."

Shar turned her attention to the chatter. "They are loosening up."

"Where will they go from here?"

"We're making plans to transfer them to other homes for unwed mothers. Reputable ones."

"I'll be taking my granddaughter with me and telling my daughter where she can shove her opinions." Alice sat down. "I don't know what more I can tell you."

"Anything about the deaths?" Shar sat back in her chair. "The high rate is what drew us here in the first place."

A shadow passed over the other woman's face. "I've only seen one body, and that one was born premature. The others just...disappeared. The girl would go into labor, Stuart would go in to deliver, we'd hear a cry, then nothing. Next thing anyone knew, Stuart said the baby died. She sold them, didn't she? This place was nothing more than a baby farm."

"I'm afraid so. The filing cabinet is full of falsified birth certificates. No parents listed, just whether the baby was boy or girl."

"A fill-in-the-blank birth. Now, I've heard everything. When are we leaving?"

"Within the week."

Everis looked up the information on Probation Officer Joe Wick and had Pinson ride along as backup. If the PO was crooked, Everis wouldn't put it past him to draw a weapon. Not if the man took bribes from Smith.

"You really think he's in cahoots with the crazy lady?" Pinson asked as they drove to the other side of town.

"I'm not assuming anything, but I am expecting the worst." Since Wick wasn't at work, according to the woman who answered the phone at the probation office, Everis drove to the man's house. A small white clapboard that had seen better days. A shiny black Mercedes sat under the carport like a silk robe over a man wasting away from disease.

"Let's get this over with," Pinson said, pushing open his door. "No one likes to be accused of a crime, but less against children. It won't be a party."

"I'm not expecting it to be."

"Of course, with me as backup, and you wearing shoes, I doubt this guy can run off." Pinson slapped his leg. "What a hoot."

"I wondered how long it would take for you to bring that up." Everis headed for the house.

"Fatherhood must really change a man." Pinson caught up with him. "Normally, I doubt you would have stopped with a little bitty piece of glass in your foot."

"I'm wearing a walking boot!" Everis glared. "It took four stitches."

Pinson roared with laughter. "I would have loved to have seen that. A middle-aged woman outrunning a fit agent like you."

"Shut up." Everis knocked on the weathered front door.

A burly man with two-day stubble on his square chin opened the door. "Yeah?"

Everis introduced themselves. "We're here about Mira Engstrom. We'd like to ask you a few questions."

"What's she done now? That girl can't keep to the conditions of her probation to save her sorry hide."

"The questions are more about why you sent her to Happiness House. May we come in?"

"I guess so. No reason to give the neighbors a show." He stepped back and opened the door further.

The house was surprisingly clean. Worn carpet and mismatched furniture, but nothing littered the coffee table or floor.

"Have a seat." Wick motioned to the sofa as he sat in a chair across from them. "Tell me what this is all about."

Pinson chose to stand, but Everis sat. "Why did you choose Happiness House?"

"Why not?" The man shrugged. "Ain't one of them

houses the same as another?"

"No sir, they're not." Everis leaned forward, his gaze glued to the man's face.

Wick's eyes flitted from him to Pinson. He drummed his fingers on the arm of the chair. "No?"

"This house is run by Rachel Smith. Sound familiar?"

"Of course. She's been plastered all over the news." The drumming of his fingers slowed. "So, you mean to tell me she's selling the babies born at that place?"

"Yes. How many girls have you sent there?"

"A few." The man's face darkened. "Why all the questions? Are you insinuating I sent those girls on purpose to help that mad woman?"

"She does seem to pay her people well, and that's a fine-looking car outside." Pinson turned away from the window. A cold smile spread across his face. "I don't know many people who leave a hundred-dollar bill on the floor." He pointed to the money poking out from under the man's chair.

Wick bent to retrieve the cash and came up with a Glock. "The two of you shouldn't have come here. Where's the honor among government workers." He leveled the weapon on Everis.

Pinson pulled his gun. "Put it down, sir."

"How much did she pay you?" Everis kept his gaze on the gun and his hand close to his own weapon.

"Ten thousand a girl." Wick grinned. "I paid cash for that car. Not many people can say that."

"You helped that woman sell infants."

"So?" He cocked his head. "What kind of life would they have with a teen mom? This way, they got adopted by people who could take care of them. The way I look at it, I helped Smith do a good deed."

Pinson took a step forward.

Wick whirled and fired.

Pinson fell.

Wick turned back to Everis.

Everis fired, his shot taking Wick in the chest. He stood over the man. "Tell me how to find her, and I'll get you medical attention." He glanced to where Wick sat slumped against the wall, eyes closed.

"Go to hell."

"That's where you're going." Everis unhooked his radio and called for an ambulance. "You holding on, Deputy?"

"Best I can. I'm thinking I'd rather step on glass like you than get shot."

"You should have worn your vest." Everis cuffed Wick, knowing the man wouldn't live long enough for the ambulance. Not with the way blood bubbled from the wound. "Where is she?"

Wick spat.

"She'd sell you out fast enough." Everis shook his head. "She's already killed two women who helped her. Your days were numbered."

The man blinked. "We've always communicated by phone. She'd leave the money on my back porch. I never saw her until her picture was on TV. The phone's on the counter in the kitchen."

Sirens wailed in the distance as Everis retrieved the phone, picking it up with a napkin and slipping it into his pocket. When he returned, Wick no longer breathed.

He sighed and stared at the man, knowing he should perform CPR, and also knowing he'd be reprimanded for not doing so. Instead, he hunkered next to Pinson and pressed the dishtowel he'd also taken from the kitchen against the hole in his shoulder.

"I think you'll live."

"Bet I'll have more than four stitches."

"I bet you're right." Everis opened the front door as the paramedics rushed toward the house. "Officer down and suspect deceased." Shar was going to kill him for getting one of her deputies shot.

Pinson must have read his mind as he was lifted onto the gurney, "The boss will get over it. She'll be glad it was me and not you. Call Candy for me, okay?" He winked as he was rolled out the door.

Chapter Fourteen

"What do you mean Pinson is in the hospital with a gunshot wound?" Shar's voice held a deadly calm.

"We went to visit the probation officer, and he got shot." Everis leaned against the hospital wall and closed his eyes. For the first time in three years, he wanted a cigarette. "He'll be fine. It's a shoulder wound. Your sister is with him now."

"I can't be there. I'm finishing things up here. We have a young lady ready to deliver any day now. A doctor finally made an appearance and said we shouldn't move her until the baby is born. She's high risk."

"I understand. I'll handle things on this end."

"Where's Vick now?"

"Dead. I shot him. I also have the phone Rachel Smith contacts him with. If we can keep his death a secret, maybe she'll phone."

"It's worth a try. I'm sorry I snapped. I've never had anyone in my office shot before."

"Again, understandable. We're all under a lot of stress." Catching sight of the doctor through the glass

113

doors, he said, "I've got to go. Pinson is out of surgery."

"You didn't say anything about surgery."

"Bye, Shar. I'll make sure he's well taken care of." He hung up and hurried inside.

"Deputy Pinson came through just fine." The doctor smiled and removed the hat he wore in surgery. "He'll be out of work for a few weeks, but good as new by week eight. The bullet lodged against the bone, but didn't shatter. He's very lucky."

"Can I see him?"

"Yes. His lady friend is in the family waiting room. No more than two at a time." He shook Everis's hand and left.

Everis made a beeline to where Candy waited and related the good news.

She burst into tears. "I was so worried. Maybe I'm not cut out for a relationship with someone in law enforcement."

"You've lived with Shar."

"That's different. She's my sister."

Everis didn't see the difference. Worry was worry. "Come on. We can go visit."

He hung back while Candy approached the bed. She slid her hand under Pinson's, then leaned forward to place a soft kiss on his lips.

His eyes fluttered open. "What a way to wake up." He glanced at Everis. "Hey."

"Hey. Sheriff's a bit miffed that you got shot. I think she blames me."

Pinson smiled. "Better than me."

"I'm headed back to Wick's to see if I can find any clues as to Smith's whereabouts. He didn't strike me as a man to enter into anything blindly."

"I'll stick around here." Pinson smirked. "Looks like I'm taking a vacation."

"And I'm going to take care of you." Candy lifted his hand to her lips.

Everis tossed them a wave. The sun was beginning its descent when he arrived at Wick's house. Good. Maybe he could snoop without the neighbors seeing too much.

Once he stepped inside the house, he turned on his flashlight and closed the front door behind him. He moved down the hall and into a home office. A laptop sat on a particle board desk. Bookshelves covered one wall. The man liked crime novels.

Everis pulled on a pair of gloves and opened the laptop. Wick hadn't had time to log out. What looked like a manuscript popped up on the screen. He scanned a few pages—eerily similar to the case of Smith taking babies. Was it possible the man used the woman for a story just as she'd used him for pregnant girls? The world was full of strange people.

A continued search brought up several files of information on Smith and her parents. More notes than Mayfield had uncovered. Not only that, but Wick had saved the link to an online market for babies. Bingo!

* * *

Rachel loaded Darcy into the car and headed for Happiness House. It was time for her weekly surveillance. "We'll just pop over and take a quick peek while it's dark, then come home and go to bed. How does that sound?"

The child smiled at her and grabbed for her hair. "Mama."

"Yes, I'm your mama."

Rachel closed the back door and climbed into the driver's seat. She still hadn't figured out a way to get Devin back, but she would. Darcy needed a big brother, something the original Darcy had lacked. Rachel had always dreamed of having a big brother, but her parents had insisted one child was enough. Not true. Every parent needed a boy and a girl.

Rachel turned off the interstate toward a road few knew about. The road took her behind the Happiness House and was well hidden by foliage. It was the perfect spot from which to spy.

Darcy slept in her car seat, leaving Rachel free to walk the twenty or so steps to her vantage point. A slender form moved past the window in Stuart's room. That wasn't the administrator. Frowning, Rachel jogged to the house and peered through the window. The sheriff! Where was that no-good Stuart? Why hadn't she warned Rachel?

She plastered her back against the wall. What to do now? She looked in again.

The sheriff had the blank birth certificates on her desk. She glanced up and said something to someone out of Rachel's sight, then sat in the office chair. How did she come to be there? Things were spiraling out of control so quickly. Rachel needed to grab Devin and leave the country.

After a few more minutes of surveillance, she determined that the agent man wasn't in attendance.

A car rolled to a stop in front of the house and a man with a black medical bag exited, followed by a woman who moved to take something out of the trunk. Did doctors still make house calls? Oh, this meant a baby was about to be born. Maybe Rachel could save one more child from this place before the night was over. Keeping low, she headed back to the car to wait.

Morning would come in a blaze of glory.

* * *

The night couldn't be more hectic. Mira wasn't the only one delivering. One other girl's infant decided to arrive two weeks early. Shar opened the door and almost hugged the doctor. "Thank you so much, Doctor Reed."

"Any time, Sheriff. As long as there are no complications, we can do this here where the girls are comfortable."

"I've put them both in the same room as per your instructions. We've hung a curtain for privacy and provided the clean rags."

"Wonderful. My nurse should be joining us momentarily. Ah, there she is." A woman in dark scrubs carried in a plastic bin of delivery supplies.

"Am I needed?" Shar hoped she wasn't.

"No, we'll call if we need you."

"I need her." Mira shouted from the bed. "I don't have a birthing coach."

"Neither do I," the other girl, Sara, said.

Shar closed her eyes and prayed for strength. "I'll stay." It was going to be a long night.

The doctor laughed. "These ladies will get a lot more demanding before we're through."

"I've never been more frightened in my entire life," Shar whispered to Becky. "I am completely out of my element."

"All we do is wait." She grinned. "I coached my sister. Took twenty hours for my niece to arrive."

"Good Lord." Shar shook her head and made a dash for the kitchen. "Alice, we need coffee. Lots of it."

"Way ahead of you." She thrust a mug into Shar's hand. "Relax. This is perfectly normal, and now that you're here, these babies will go where they belong."

"I hope so." Shar breathed in strength from the coffee, then slowly made her way back to the birthing room.

"I've given them epidurals," Doctor Reed said. "They won't feel a thing in a few minutes."

"Thank goodness." Mira fell back onto her pillows. "I'm never having a baby again."

"Come now. You'll meet some fine young man and change your mind someday," the nurse said. "It's all worth it when you hold the little one in your arms."

"I'm giving it to the sheriff."

Shar dropped her mug. It shattered on the wooden floor, splattering her pant legs with hot coffee. "Excuse me?"

"You'll be a better mother than my sister. I want you to take my baby."

Tears sprang to Shar's eyes. Coming to Happiness House had broken down all her defenses. She couldn't put her sheriff mask on if she tried. Not here. Not when surrounded by young women who needed her.

"I, uh…" she whirled and dashed from the room like a coward. She pulled her phone from her pocket and called Everis. "One of the girls wants to give me her baby. What do I do?"

"Adopt it?" He laughed. "You said you wanted a child. You'd make a wonderful mother."

"I'm scared spitless. Any news?" She'd think about a baby later.

"I found the website to the black market. I'm arranging for a couple of agents to charade as adoptive parents. Hopefully that will put Smith into our hands."

"We'll go gung ho again, once I get out of here. Have you ever had a case like this one?"

"Where seemingly normal people willingly worked for a psycho to earn a few bucks? No."

Shar leaned against the wall and lightly banged her head. "What's happening to my town?"

"The evil of the world creeps in everywhere."

Becky waved to her from the door of the birthing room.

"I've got to go. I'll call you later."

"Think about the girl's offer, Shar. You might regret saying no." He laughed and hung up.

Shar grinned and rejoined the others.

Mira held out her hand. "It's coming. It's coming right now. I'm scared."

"You'll do just fine." Shar took her hand. "You're bringing a miracle into the world."

"Doctor, this one is crowning." The nurse pulled his attention to Sara.

"Well, isn't this fine? Two babies at once." He bustled back and forth, determining that Mira was doing better than Sara. "Sheriff, keep an eye out. Let me know when I need to catch me a baby."

Shar's mouth dried up. "What?"

"Keep an eye on the baby. Tell me when you can see its head."

Mercy. Shar moved to the foot of the bed. "You mean like this?" She pointed.

"You'll have to take over, sheriff. I'm busy over here. You had training at the academy, right?"

"Yes, but I never expected to actually use it." She forced a smile at Mira. "Okay, I'll, uh…"

Mira gave a grunt and pushed a beautiful boy into Shar's hands.

"It's a boy. Oh, my gosh. What do I do?"

Becky handed her a towel. "Wrap him up in this until the nurse and doctor are finished."

The baby's features blurred through Shar's tears. He opened his little mouth and let out a cry that seemed too strong for one so tiny. "Would you like to hold him, Mira?"

"No, just show him to me. He's yours." She grinned. "I make pretty babies, don't I."

"The best."

Within minutes, another cry joined in. This baby was placed on its young mother's chest. "Another boy," the doctor called out. "Now, let's make sure they're healthy."

Half an hour later, everyone slept except Shar. Instead, she sat in the front room in a rocking chair and stared into the face of the child she hoped would one day be hers. Of course, she wanted him. He'd slid right into her hands like a gift. "I'm a mother." She caressed his face and let the tears fall.

"What's wrong?" Becky leaned in the doorway.

"I'm happy and scared out of my mind. I don't know anything about babies. What if the state doesn't let me keep him?"

"Why wouldn't they?" She stared down at him. "He's gorgeous. What's his name?"

"I can't believe I'm saying this, but I always wanted to name a son after my father, scoundrel that he was. I'm going to call him Robert."

"I guess we're done here."

"I guess we are. Tomorrow we'll start moving the other girls, and Mira and Sara are free to go…wherever. That makes me sad." Mira would go back to the streets, and Sara back to foster care. Sometimes life was so unfair. At least, Shar could do her best to help the baby she held, and she wouldn't give up hope on finding help for Mira.

Chapter Fifteen

Rachel made sure Darcy slept secure in her car seat before bolting for the house. It was the hour right before dawn when the world was at its darkest, and people slept.

Easing open a back window that never fully closed, she climbed into the house. Light snoring came from the front room. A peek inside showed the sheriff fast asleep with an infant in her lap. It would be too risky to take that one.

Rachel tiptoed up the stairs to the birthing room. Both beds were occupied. In a bassinet near the bed on the right lay a beautiful baby. There was no time to see whether it was a boy or a girl. She quietly scooped up the baby and backed away.

Too easy. No one ever suspected a person to sneak in under the nose of law enforcement.

She climbed back out the way she came and laid the baby on a patch of grass well away from the house before retrieving the gas can she'd brought along. A splash here and there, a tossed match, and flames flickered to life and fed hungrily. Rachel laughed and tacked a note to a nearby tree.

She lifted the baby and strolled back to her car as if she didn't have a care in the world.

Shar opened her eyes and gazed down at the baby in her lap. He'd woken to eat every two hours, and since Mira refused to breastfeed a baby she wasn't keeping, Shar had the privilege of getting up with him. Now, her neck ached, her arm was asleep under Robby's head, and she couldn't be happier.

She stood and took a deep breath. Did she smell smoke? She hurried to the kitchen. As she stepped inside the empty room, the smoke detectors started wailing. Keeping a firm grip on the baby, she dashed into the hall. Flames ate through the back wall.

"Fire!" She raced up the stairs and banged on doors. "Let's go. The house is on fire. It'll block us up here if you don't hurry."

"What?" Becky stepped out of her room.

"Fire. Help me."

"Go get Sara. I'll hurry the others on."

Shar nodded and made a dash for the birthing room. "Get up, girls. Now." She turned to the bassinet. Empty. It didn't take her long to see that Sara didn't have her baby. "Where's your son?"

The girl coughed. "In the bassinet."

"No, he isn't. Let's go. Maybe someone took him out to give you a break." Dread filled Shar from her toes to her head. Her eyes teared from the increasing smoke. What had taken the smoke alarms so long to go off? "Mira." She shook the girl. "Wake up."

"Go away."

"We're going to burn." She yanked the blankets off the girl as Sara stumbled from the room. "If you don't get up, I'll leave you, Mira. I'll take the baby and go."

"Do I smell smoke?" She sat up, eyes wide.

"Yes." Shar grabbed her arm and dragged her along.

The smoke was so thick on the bottom floor, visibility was almost nil. Doing her best to keep the swaddling blanket over Robby's face, Shar clutched the handrail and slowly made her way down, leaving Mira to hold onto her belt.

"Shar!" Becky's voice cut through the roar of the fire.

"Here. On the stairs."

"You can't come this way. Go back up. The fire trucks are coming."

Go back up? Shar's stomach turned to liquid.

"I can't." Mira clutched her arm.

"We don't have a choice. Get low to the floor." A fit of coughing seized Shar. Already her throat was raw.

Mira dropped to her hands and knees.

With one hand occupied with the baby, Shar could only hunch over. She shuffled along the hall, using her free hand to run along the wall to guide her. She could only pray Mira followed as she'd ordered. She moved back to the birthing room.

Thankfully, Mira quickly joined her.

"Shut the door. Put one of the blankets along the crack to keep as much smoke out as possible. I'm going to open the window." Shar laid the baby on the bed and shoved the window open, taking in huge gulps of fresh air. She turned and picked Robby back up, bringing him to the window. They were safe for a while.

"How long before the trucks arrive?" Mira asked, hanging out the window. "I think I can shimmy down that trellis."

"No. It looks like it's a hundred-years old." They weren't that desperate yet, although she might reconsider the climb if the trucks didn't arrive soon.

A movement at the tree line caught her attention. Rachel Smith waved and melted into the shadows. Shar reached for the gun that wasn't on her hip. She'd seen no reason to wear while helping deliver two babies.

"I can do this." Mira leaned out and grabbed the trellis.

"No." Shar pulled her back. "I see lights."

A fire truck and ambulance wailed to a stop in front of the house. Within minutes, a ladder was propped against the house.

"Now, Mira." Shar glanced at the door. Fingers of fire had poked through. "Hurry."

By now, Robby's screams had joined the noise of the fire and trucks outside, or maybe Shar hadn't heard him until then. Either way, she was more frightened and felt more helpless than at any other time in her life. Before, she'd had only herself to watch out for, maybe Candy, but now there was the baby in her arms, Everis and Brian.

"Come on, Sheriff." Mira glanced up from halfway down the ladder.

"You don't need to tell me twice." Shar swung her leg over and started the difficult one-handed climb to the ground. When her feet touched dirt, she wanted to kiss every pebble.

She handed Robby to a paramedic. "He was in the house for quite a while. Please, take good care of him."

The medic glanced down. "Newborn?"

"Yes, he's my son." Shar grinned and headed to the group of frightened girls.

When Everis heard on the police scanner that Happiness House was on fire, he'd called Candy to babysit and sped away. All he could think about was Shar. Was she okay? Were the girls alright?

He pulled to a stop off to the side of the firetruck and stared through the window at the inferno in front of him. A group of girls stood well away from the blaze.

Shar stepped out from behind the ambulance, and Everis rushed over to her. Without a word, he pulled her into a fierce hug. "You scare me to death; do you know that?"

"I have to admit to being terrified."

"We didn't think she'd make it out," Becky said, walking up to them. "I got the others out, but Shar stayed behind to argue with a stubborn girl. The firemen brought her and the baby down the ladder."

"Baby?" He held her at arm's length. "When do I get to meet your son?"

"In a minute." She stared into his face. "Smith was here. She took the other baby born last night."

"What? How?"

Shar shrugged. "She snuck in and took the baby. Easy as that. The mother slept in the same room, yet she still managed." She motioned her head to a sobbing young woman. "Two people in that room and yet…"

"She's an evil spirit that comes and goes at will." Everis headed to where the crying young girl sat on a gurney.

She raised a tear-stained face. "Are you going to get my baby back?"

"I'm going to do my best." Which, so far, wasn't much at all. For years, the Smiths had carried on with their illegal adoptions and perfected their scheme over time. In order to be brought down, Rachel Smith would have to make a mistake. A big one.

Shar took his hand and pulled his gaze to the baby in her arms. "Meet Robert, Robby for short." Tears shimmered in her eyes.

"He's beautiful." Two wonderful things had happened from the ashes of chaos. He'd found Brian, and Shar now had a child. They were lucky. Now, they needed to help repair the damage done by the Smith family.

Shar handed the baby to Becky. "Smith was standing over there while I stood in the burning house waiting to be rescued." She led him to the edge of the trees. "She stood here and waved, then left. She's enjoying this. It's become a game to her, Everis."

He noted a paper tacked to a tree and read aloud, "Give me my son, and this will all end." Her son? "Is she talking about Brian?" Hell would freeze over before he would put his child back into her hands.

"A car was parked here," Shar said, studying a set of tracks in the dirt. "Standard issue, I think. Footprints, etc. She'd parked here, taken the baby, and left me to burn."

He wiped a smudge of soot from her face. "I'm glad you didn't. Mayfield found the black- market site on the web. The department is sending a couple to go undercover as adoptive parents."

Her expression hardened. "I was hoping to be the one to capture her."

"You and me both, but we're too recognizable."

"We'll just have to make sure we're close enough to the fake parents to be a part of her arrest." She turned back to the house, or what was left of it.

The once beautiful plantation-style building was nothing but charred beams and smoldering ashes. Thankfully, no one was killed. "Let's get to the office and formulate a plan."

"I need to call Child Protective Services and make sure I can take Bobby home with me, then I need to find someone to watch him."

Everis chuckled. "Welcome to parenthood. As young as he is, why not bring him to the office with you?"

"Great idea." An hour later, Shar carried a baby carrier into the office and set her son on the conference table. She glanced at Everis. "Let's get this woman."

"Agent Valdez and Agent Mason will be our adoptive parents. They're going by the name of Mr. and Mrs. Worth. You and I will handle all online communication," Everis said. "Once we have a time and place to make the trade of child and cash, they'll step in."

"After the horrors of Lars Townsend and his online murdering, I thought I'd seen everything." Shar glanced at the baby. "But to find out how big child trafficking is has settled in my heart like a stone. Smith can't be the only one doing this." She raised her gaze to Everis. "How many more in how many states?"

"More than we can take down." As much as each failure haunted him, Everis knew it was impossible to put away all the bad guys. More popped up all the time. In small, out-of-the-way towns like Highland Springs, someone with evil intent could move in, put on a pleasant persona and literally get away with murder.

Everyone knew everyone in small towns, but

usually took a person at face value. That's how people like Lars Townsend and Rachel Smith were able to do such evil deeds before being discovered. Some places attracted the bad, and Everis feared the beautiful Highland Springs might be such a place, despite the sheriff who loved her town.

Chapter Sixteen

Sluggish from lack of sleep, Shar poured her third cup of coffee since coming into the office. That wasn't counting the drink she'd bought from the coffee shop on her way in. After heading home the night before, then having to shower to get the smell of smoke out of her hair and soot off her skin, Bobby had woken twice in the five hours Shar had left to sleep. Today, Candy begged to watch him.

"You look dead on your feet." Mayfield leaned against the doorjamb. "Heard you almost got cooked and gained a kid all in the same night."

"It was definitely one for the history books." She headed for the conference room. "Are we ready to put out feelers to adopt?"

"Yes, I've got the profiles set—"

Amber clip-clopped down the tiled hall toward them. "There's a woman out front you're going to want to talk to, Sheriff."

Shar rubbed her face. "Put her in my office. I'll be right there."

"Go ahead. I'll catch you up when you're done. Everis said he'd be in later. Something about a call to headquarters."

Sometimes Shar forgot Everis actually worked out of another place. When crime called him to Highland Springs, he fit in as if he'd always been there. One of these days, headquarters might send someone else, and nothing would be the same.

After adding a packet of creamer to her coffee, she carried the mug to her office. A woman sat across from her desk. At her feet was an infant carrier.

"Good morning. I'm Sheriff Camenetti. Can I get you something to drink?"

"No, thank you." The woman heaved a sigh. "Early this morning as I was headed to my massage therapist, a woman stopped me. She asked if I wanted a baby. She said she knew I did, and she had one for me." She twisted the tie on her blouse. "Well, I was quite taken back. She sold this darling child to me for whatever cash I had in my wallet, which happened to be $121.45. I didn't know what else to do but come here."

Shar stood frozen for several seconds, then pushed a photo of Rachel Smith across her desk. "Was it this woman?"

"Yes. This infant isn't doing well, Sheriff." She lifted it from the carrier and placed the teen Sara's newborn into Shar's arms.

The baby had a yellowish shade to its skin and seemed weak. "Have you fed her?"

"No, I don't exactly carry formula around with me." She stood.

"Thank you, Ms—"

"Armstrong. You're welcome. I'm glad to help." She peered one more time at the baby. "I do so want a child, but not this way. Let me know if this little one is available." She flashed a grin and left.

Shar immediately called the hospital, who promised to send someone for the baby, then called the shelter where Sara had been taken. They promised to take the mother to her child.

One thing taken care of. Shar booted up her computer. Several emails required her attention—some complaints on noise, which she would assign to Mayfield, and a score of calls to the silent witness line with supposed sightings of Smith. Most were probably nothing, but they would all need to be checked, which would take time they didn't have. With Pinson in the hospital and Becky back in Little Rock, the sheriff's office was once again shorthanded.

"Good morning." Everis strolled into the office looking as good as if he'd had a full night's sleep. "How was your first night as a mother?"

"I'm exhausted." She grinned. "You look good, though."

"My child sleeps through the night." He sat in the chair vacated by Ms. Armstrong and glanced at the baby carrier, then back at Shar.

"The baby looks like it has jaundice. It's the one stolen from Happiness House. I've called the hospital and the mother, and the baby was sold for a little over a hundred dollars to a woman on the street." Shar took a deep breath. "That's been my morning."

"Wow. Busy."

"Not to mention," she glanced back at her computer screen, "twelve sightings of Smith that need to be checked out, five reports of noise disturbances from local teens terrorizing the neighborhood, and I need to be spending time pretending to be someone desperately wanting to adopt." She phoned Amber to have Mayfield meet her in the conference room.

She stood and headed for the door, lifting the baby carrier on her way. "Everything okay at headquarters?" she asked, glancing over her shoulder.

"Yeah, just something I'm working on." He gave a secretive smile, then made shooing motions with his hands.

"Fine. Keep your secrets." He'd tell her eventually. He always did.

Mayfield already sat at the conference table, laptop open in front of him. "As I was saying earlier," his gaze flicked to the baby carrier. "This is the strangest law enforcement office I've ever been in. There's either a dog or a child here."

"We are a bit unorthodox. The hospital is sending someone for this little darling. I'll be right back." Shar headed to the front office. "Amber, this package will be picked up shortly. Hopefully, she won't wake up hungry before it happens." She flashed a grin at the wide-eyed receptionist and rejoined the men.

"I've got the couple's photo posted on the site," Mayfield was saying, "and made a point in stating they didn't have a preference in looks or gender. That's pretty much it. All we do now is wait for an answer. If Smith dropped off the baby she just stole, we might have missed the boat on this."

"Meaning, she's moved on." Shar hoped not. Missouri hadn't caught her. If they didn't, she might end up in Montana next. Plenty of open spaces for her to hide.

"I don't think so." Everis leaned back. "That note she left us told me she wants Brian. She won't leave until she has him."

"Which won't be easy with Goliath guarding." Shar sat down and reached for her less than half full coffee cup. "Still, we should up the protection."

"I have an agent watching the house."

* * *

Rachel stared unblinking at the agent's rented house until her eyes started to dry out. It didn't take a rocket scientist to see the agent in the black suburban watching the house. Nor did it matter that the giant dog padded everywhere Devin went. Rachel would find a way in and take back her child.

Her phone dinged, signaling a post on her site. Wonderful. She'd need a new child since the last one wasn't as healthy as he should have been. Nope, she couldn't sell a yellow baby.

She studied the new profile of eager parents. They looked nice enough. Dark-haired, brown-eyed man, blue-eyed, blond woman. She could pretty much snag any child, and they could pass it off as their own. She liked the easy ones.

"Let's go to the grocery to do a little shopping." She pulled a red wig over her dark hair, donned a pair of coke-bottle glasses, and put in some fake upper teeth that distorted the shape of her mouth. She was no dummy. She knew her face was plastered across every television in Arkansas and bordering states.

She also wasn't stupid enough to go shopping any longer in Highland Springs. She drove to Fort Smith and cruised a lower income area of the city. Here was where children needed saving from parents who didn't pay them enough attention.

Having Darcy was the best camouflage. Women

would glance at her, smile, and continue their shopping. No one cast more than a cursory glance at Rachel. She kept a smile on her face and kept searching.

By the meat counter, a woman leaned over a display of roasts, her back to a cart holding a sweet little child. Rather than being hooked to the seat, the carrier was simply placed in the back. A quick lift, place, and a scurry down the next aisle. Rachel was almost to the door before she heard the woman's scream.

No one watched as she pushed her cart containing an infant and a toddler out the door. Nor did anyone stop her as she loaded them into her car. After all, who suspected such a plain-looking woman with two children as being The Child Saver?

Everis watched as the photo of an infant girl around the age of six months was posted to the profile of the Worths. The very baby sent out on an Amber alert from Hot Springs.

"Why aren't women taking this seriously?" He scrunched his shoulders in a vain attempt to relieve the tension locked there. "How many times do they have to hear not to turn their back on their child for even a moment? Is it really that hard to shop with the cart in *front* of you?" He wished for the power to set a law in motion that stated women would be fined if they lost their child.

"Don't be cruel. Smith is the one at fault here, not the mothers." Shar stared at the screen. "At least, we'll get this one back to her mother. We've been chasing Smith for less than a month. So much has happened that it seems a lot longer. We're making progress, Everis."

"When did you become the positive one?"

She laughed. "I guess you rubbed off on me. I did make you a promise."

"True. I'm holding you to it, too."

"We will catch her." She smiled.

"Hey!" Mayfield burst into the conference room. "I truly am a computer wizard. I found a cabin owned by the Smiths that is believed to be vacant. Who wants to bet our creep is living there? It's only thirty minutes away, right on the border of us and Missouri. No address, just coordinates."

"Let's go." Everis grabbed his gun belt and made a beeline for the jeep, calling for backup from Little Rock as they went. "Text me those coordinates."

Ten minutes later, they sat snarled in traffic. "Seriously?" Everis cut Shar a glance. "Mind going off-road?"

"We have four-wheel drive. Hang on." She put flashing lights on the roof, turned the wheel and then bounced the jeep into a ditch and out the other side. "Hopefully, no morons will try the same thing."

"Too late. A minivan is stuck. Don't stop. They aren't injured." Everis shook his head and he watched through the rear window as several boys in soccer gear exited the van. "Someone is going to miss their game."

"They ought to know better than to try and follow a vehicle with flashing lights."

Everis grabbed the handle over the door and held on as Shar veered back into the ditch and out again before finding an area of ground smooth enough to increase their speed and rocket down the side of the road while other cars sat still.

He craned his neck to see a fender bender. Highway patrol and an ambulance were on scene. "No need for us to stop." He glanced at the GPS on his phone. "Turn here."

"Where?"

"Here."

She yanked the wheel down a path. "You're going to have to pay for a paint job. This isn't a road. It's barely a trail."

He bit his tongue as he started to answer, but was cut off short as they hit a hole. "Stop up ahead and wait for backup. I don't want to go in alone. The more we have, the less chance of her getting away again."

"Unless she isn't there, and we're blocking the road she uses to get there."

"Headlights."

They stared as a police SUV stopped behind them. An officer got out, weapon drawn and approached the jeep.

Everis showed his badge. "How many are you?"

"There's two of us, sir."

Did no one take this woman seriously? "It's not enough."

Chapter Seventeen

The four of them moved down the path. Shar kept her gun ready and her senses on high alert. Every contact, every sighting, brought them closer to bringing Smith to justice.

None of them spoke. The only sound was the breeze rustling leaves and the occasional squawk of a bird as it darted away from them. The woods were normally Shar's friend, but today they seemed malevolent, lying in wait to devour her.

Everis made silent signals for them to spread out. He went one way with an officer, Shar the other. This was a time she was more than happy to let him take the lead.

A year ago, she'd have fought to keep control. Was she slipping in her job as sheriff? Had the crimes, now so prevalent in Highland Springs, proven she wasn't good enough after all?

She stopped and hunkered behind a thick cluster of bushes and stared at a cabin that looked ready to fall down at any time. No smoke came from the chimney. Being daylight, she wasn't able to see through the windows. She motioned for the officer to stay and, staying low, circled to the back of the cabin, using trees as coverage.

The faint cry of a baby drifted through an open window, followed by hushing sounds. Shar inched closer, plastering her back against the outer wall. Turning her head, she peered through the window.

Smith cradled the infant against her shoulder and hummed a tuneless lullaby. When the baby quieted, she laid the little girl on a quilt thrown over a tattered sofa. Showtime.

Shar hurried back to the others. "Smith is there with a child. She appears unarmed, but not seeing a weapon doesn't mean there isn't one."

"Agreed." Everis motioned for the others to move closer. "Do not shoot. We don't want to risk hurting the child."

"Smith won't risk the little girl. She was gentle with her." Shar squared her shoulders. "I'll move in first and try to draw her outside."

"No, I'll do it." Everis shot out a hand to stop her.

"I'm less intimidating." Shar grabbed a bullhorn from the pack Everis carried on his back. "Rachel Smith, this is Sheriff Camenetti. Come out with your hands up."

"You must think I'm brainless." Smith shouted back. "Don't come any closer. I've a child in here."

"Leave the child and come out. Cooperation will help things."

"Right. You're all fools." She slammed shutters into place over the windows.

Shar glanced at Everis. A muscle ticked in his jaw.

"We need backup," he said. "Radio it in. This could get ugly very fast."

Shar hoped not. A shootout never ended well. "Looks like we wait." She leaned against a tree, one knee bent and watched the house. Although hidden, she had a clear view.

Smith had locked the cabin down tight. Not even a sniper could get a clear shot if it came down to shooting. They'd have to wait her out.

Her phone vibrated. She glanced at the screen and smiled. Mira had relinquished her parental rights, and Shar's lawyer could now start the adoption proceedings. The state had agreed to leave Robby under Shar's guardianship. It was becoming very real.

She glanced back at the cabin. Did Smith really believe the child inside was hers? If so, Shar could understand the woman's determination to prevent them from returning the baby to its mother.

"Smith, the sheriff again. Does the child need anything? There's no need for her to suffer."

"I am quite capable of caring for her."

Shar shrugged in Everis's direction. "Other officers will be arriving, Rachel. It's best you surrender now and turn the child over."

"She's my daughter!"

Shar lowered the horn. "Can anyone get a glimpse of her?"

Everis shook his head. "It's dark. I think she's yelling through that crack in the window. We need to get closer. She won't come out willingly."

"There's a wide gap in back between the door frame. We might be able to get a shot that way." Shar headed around back again.

Did that stupid sheriff really think she would give

up? She stared down at her baby. Not a chance. She still needed to take back her son, so she could leave the state. Maybe go down to Mexico or north to Canada. Somewhere she could start a new life with her children.

A rock clattered behind the cabin. Rachel cursed and reached above the cupboard for her gun. Couldn't leave it where Darcy could get her hands on it, now could she? That was the difference between her and the birth parent. Rachel thought about what was best for her child.

She hurried to the bedroom and glanced through a space in the shutter. A police officer darted from tree to tree. Idiot. Rachel knew this land like the back of her hand. She knew every tree, bush, and shadow. There was no way anyone could sneak up on her.

Returning to the living room, she lifted the sleeping Darcy and put her in the hole under the trapdoor. Her father had made an escape hatch a long time ago when the cabin had been their headquarters before the big house. Rachel had a way out when things turned nasty. For now, it was the best place to keep Darcy safe.

Rachel moved through the house pouring gasoline in every corner and across every surface. Torching the place would slow down those outside and give her the opportunity to escape. But first, there was something she'd been wanting to do.

She set the book of matches on the coffee table and headed back to the bedroom. Taking careful aim with her gun through a knothole in the shutter, she squeezed the trigger.

*　*　*

Everis froze as the shot rang out.

Shar bent at the waist, grabbed her midsection, and

crumbled to the ground.

The other two officers returned fire.

Everis sprinted across the yard to Shar. Grabbing her under the arms, he dragged her to the safety of the trees. "Talk to me, sweetheart."

"I'm fine. Really." Blood spread between her fingers. "Get Smith."

He radioed for backup, then pulled her hands away from her wound. "I need to stop the bleeding."

"Don't let her get away again." She slapped his hand away.

He nodded, shifting from concerned man to committed agent. "Don't die on me." He raced toward the cabin. A small explosion knocked him off his feet. Flames shot from the windows.

Struggling to get back on his feet, he trudged toward the cabin. "Smith!" He yanked open the backdoor. The fire burned too hot for him to enter. How could she have killed herself and the child?

Dashing back to Shar, he radioed for a chopper. Smith had to have tricked them. He couldn't believe she'd kill herself and the child. It went against what little he knew of her. "Get a chopper circling this cabin. She's out there somewhere." Instinct told him so.

Shar had propped herself against a tree trunk. "The cabin's on fire?"

"Yes, but I don't—"

"I agree. The big house had an underground tunnel. I bet this one does too."

"Great minds think alike. I've called for a chopper." He removed his shirt and pressed it against her wound. She gasped, but he didn't pull away. "You're as pale as a ghost."

143

CYNTHIA HICKEY

"I'm not feeling very well." She leaned her head back and closed her eyes.

"Open your eyes, Shar. Look at me." He patted her cheek.

Her eyes opened in slits. "Take care of Robby."

"Take care of him yourself." He blinked back tears and cleared his throat. "I don't want to be here without you, Camenetti. Hold on. For me and Robby." He kept pressure against her stomach. Where was the ambulance?

His radio crackled. "We've spotted the suspect fleeing on foot south of you. She's headed toward a logging road. There's nowhere to set down the chopper."

"Then get over here. Officer down." Everis kept his gaze locked on Shar's face. He wouldn't lose her. Somehow, someway, Smith was going to pay.

* * *

Two hours after Shar was wheeled into surgery, the doctor approached the waiting room. Everis stood, putting a hand on Candy's shoulder as she sat with Robby in her lap and Brian in the chair beside her. The doctor wouldn't be smiling unless it was good news, right?

"Our sheriff is one tough lady." He removed his surgical cap. The bullet nicked an artery, but we've repaired the damage. She did require a few pints of blood. She'll be fine in a few weeks and have a scar as a conversation piece."

Everis gripped the doctor's hand. "Thank you. When can we see her?"

"You can go one at a time now, but the infant can't go into ICU."

144

"You go," Candy said, tears shimmering in her eyes. "Shar would want to know her son is fine. I'll see her later."

"Are you sure?"

She nodded. "Go. Don't let her wake up alone."

Everis didn't need more coaxing. He rushed to Shar's room and paused in the doorway.

Her face seemed unnaturally pale against her mane of dark hair. Her lashes cast dark shadows on her cheeks. She looked as if she were waiting to be placed in her final resting place. Only the rise and fall of her chest and the gentle hiss of the oxygen testified to her still being among the living.

He pulled the salmon-colored chair closer to the bed and sat down, then took her hand in his. He remained that way for a long time, ignoring the nurses that came and went. There were some decisions to be made. Ones that would affect not only his future, but possibly Shar's as well. He just wasn't sure he was ready to take the required step.

Lifting her hand to his lips, he placed a kiss in her palm. His life had changed dramatically a year ago when he'd seen this beautiful woman across a barroom dance floor. She looked the least like a sheriff of anyone he knew, and was one of the best he'd ever met. It wasn't until meeting her that Everis began to doubt whether he wanted to remain in Little Rock.

Her eyes fluttered, then opened, pulling him from his thoughts. "I'm alive."

"Yes, thank God, you are." He leaned over and kissed her forehead. "How do you feel?"

"Like I've been shot." The corner of her mouth twitched. "Thank you for coming." Her eyes closed.

He laughed. "As if anything could have stopped me." He leaned back in his chair and prepared himself to sit there all night if need be.

Mayfield stood in the doorway. "Smith got away. We have no idea what type of vehicle or in what direction she went."

"We'll find her again."

The deputy wrinkled his brow. "How can you be so sure?"

"Because she wants my son." Everis speared Mayfield a glance. "Go check on him, please. He's in the waiting room with Candy."

"Sure thing." He cast a look at Shar. "She okay?"

"She'll survive." Everis rested his head in his hand. "Pinson?"

"Ranting to be released and wanting to see the sheriff with his own eyes." Mayfield took one more glimpse of Shar, then left, hopefully to check on those in the waiting room.

What could they do to make sure Smith didn't get away again? First, find her. But no trap they'd set had captured her. The woman was a rat with so many hidey-holes she could be anywhere. Especially if she really had as much money as Everis thought she did.

With them gaining on her every day, he didn't think she'd grab more children. Instead, she'd be planning on a way to get to Brian. Everis needed to come up with a way to prevent his son disappearing, and also put Rachel Smith behind bars.

In the hallway, a nurse complained to another that she rarely saw her husband since she'd given him his birthday present. Everis grinned and dialed his office. "Can I get a drone?"

Chapter Eighteen

The sheriff still lived? Rachel stomped across the apartment floor, only quieting her steps when her downstairs neighbor banged on the floor. The landlord had been happy enough to rent the dump when offered enough money. He didn't seem to care who she was or take a second glance at her signature on the lease. Money could buy a person anything. Even if said person was a fugitive.

Rachel smiled and sat on the world's ugliest sofa, a pea-green with brown stripes, and turned on the thirty-seven-inch television. She'd thought about trying for a more upscale place, but the managers in more ritzy apartments were harder to bribe.

She scowled as reporters flashed photos of the sheriff leaving the hospital. Behind her was her sister holding the black baby boy. Rachel leaned forward. Behind them was the agent holding the hand of Rachel's son.

How dare he parade the boy in front of her like that? He taunted her, begged her to meet him face-to-face for a final showdown. "Oh, we'll see each other, Mr. Agent. Oh, yes, we will."

The agent stared at the camera as if he knew she watched him. She wasn't sure, but it seemed as if he mouthed the words, "He's mine." Surely, not. He wouldn't challenge her that way, would he? She'd proven multiple times that she was a better adversary than he had ever come across.

She switched off the television. Everything in her wanted to barge in, guns blazing, and save her son. Wisdom told her she needed to lay low for a while. She glanced at Darcy. It would be a good bonding time for her and her daughter.

* * *

A week later, Shar groaned and lowered herself into a recliner. "I'm not getting up all day." She never knew a body could hurt so much.

Candy laughed. "Here's Robby. You'll have to get up and take care of him. I have to go to work. Everis will be in and out, he said. Since you can't lift over ten pounds, and this little guy weighs eight, you'll be just fine."

"Yes, I am." She held out her arms. "I've missed him."

"Don't overdo it, Shar," Candy tossed over her shoulder as she headed for the door. "I can't be your full-time nurse."

"We don't need a nurse, do we?" Shar ran her forefinger down the baby's nose. Her phone rang, and she realized she'd left it on the kitchen counter. "Maybe we do." After a bit of struggling to stand without dropping the baby or pulling out her stitches, she reached her phone. "Sheriff Camenetti."

"I need you to come get me."

"Mira?"

"Who else? I'm in Eureka Springs."

"Why do I need to come get you?"

"I got busted shoplifting. I told the cops I live with you."

Shar leaned against the counter. "That would be a lie, Mira."

"I ain't got nowhere to go. It's either you come get me or I go to jail. Do you know what happens in jail?"

Shar sighed. "I can't come get you, but I can send Agent Hayes. Try to stay out of trouble until then."

"Yeah, thanks." Click.

"I guess we're having a houseguest," she whispered to the baby after calling Everis. "Let's pray she doesn't want you back." Since the papers weren't finalized, that little fear consistently niggled at her mind. It wouldn't be difficult to prove Mira unfit, but it would definitely slow down the process.

Shar put Robby in his crib and shuffled to the guest room. By the time she'd changed the bedding, exhaustion wracked her body, and sweat poured down her back. This could very well be considered overdoing it.

Her phone rang again. This time it was Mayfield. "Hey, Mark."

"We've had a spotting of Smith on the south side. I'm heading over there to speak with the pharmacy owner."

"Thank you for not waiting for orders."

He laughed. "You're down, Everis is gone, and Pinson hasn't received his medical release yet. There isn't anyone to ask."

"Let me know what you find out." She hung up and shuffled back to her chair. Mayfield was right. He was all that was left functioning in a sheriff's office that was already minimally staffed.

What made Shar believe she could be both sheriff and a mother? There would be times she'd have to miss work because Robby was ill, or times like this when she was the one needing attention. What if she were killed in the line of duty? Sure, Candy would be more than willing to be guardian, but a child needed a parent whose life wasn't in danger on a regular basis.

She rested her head against the chair back. She loved her town and her job. She'd fallen in love with Robby. Maybe it was her pain meds talking, but why were decisions so hard to make?

She woke to a knock on the door. Holding her arm tight against her side, she opened the door to let Everis, Brian, and a sullen Mira in.

"Ah, you must have lectured her on the drive," Shar said, grinning.

"I did." Everis placed a soft kiss on her cheek.

"Yeah, like he was my dad or something." Mira headed for the kitchen, Brian running after her. Someone wasn't intimidated by the sour-faced teen. "What's to eat around here?"

Robby started to cry from his room.

Everis steered Shar back to her chair. "Sit. I can handle the teen and the infant. Brian isn't going anywhere, either. Not until this case is solved."

"Are you sure?"

He grinned. "I've faced down serial killers; I think I can do this."

"Good luck." Shar leaned back and closed her eyes. She strongly doubted he would be in one piece after an hour with Mira. If she weren't so tired, she'd sit back and enjoy the show.

Everis rubbed his hands together. He could do this.

Ignoring the banging of cupboards coming from the kitchen, he headed down the hallway, following the increasing shrieks of an unhappy baby. He pushed open the door and stared into the crib. "You sure do have a lot of hair, little guy." He lifted Robby. The cries immediately stopped.

"Let's get you changed, then fed." See how easy it was?

He gagged the moment he opened the diaper. "What in the world does your mommy feed you?" His stomach heaved, and he turned away, taking in great gulps of air. Finally, he composed himself, held his breath and changed the diaper. Okay. Feeding time. Carrying the infant in the crook of his arm like a football, he hurried to the kitchen.

Disaster had struck. Not only was every inch of counter space covered with flour, but Brian's dark hair looked as if it had snowed.

He grinned. "Cookies, daddy."

Everis raised an eyebrow at Mira. "Do you know how?"

She shrugged. "How hard can it be?" She glanced at Robby. "Ever taken care of a newborn before?"

"Touché. How hard can it be?" He headed for the refrigerator and pulled out a half gallon of milk.

"Formula, smart agent man." Mira pointed to a can on top of the fridge. "Read the directions, or you'll be wearing whatever he drinks."

"Robby. The sheriff named him Robert after her father."

She curled his nose. "A white boy's name. He ought to be called Jamal or Devron."

Everis took down the can of formula and tried measuring while holding the baby. Mira sighed dramatically and took the can from him and a bottle from the dish drainer next to the sink. A couple of minutes later, Everis sat in a kitchen chair and fed four ounces to a content infant. There. That wasn't too bad.

When the bottle was empty, he straightened Robby. The baby's eyes widened and formula projectiled from his mouth. Everis gagged and held him at arm's length.

Mira waved a wooden spoon in his direction. "You're supposed to burp a baby halfway through their feeding."

"Help me." Everis swallowed past the bile in his throat.

"I'll take him." Shar stepped into the kitchen and took her son. "Go shower. Toss your shirt in the washing machine." Her mouth twitched.

"Do not laugh." He peeled off his shirt and froze as both females stared. "What?"

Shar glanced at Mira. "Uh, nothing."

"Nothing?" Mira waved her hand at her face. "You're hot, agent man."

Heat rose up his neck, and his gaze clashed with Mira's. He leaned close. "Don't stare at me like that," he warned. "The look in your eyes is an invitation for a kiss if I've ever seen one. Very unprofessional, Sheriff."

"Go on. We'll keep an eye on Brian." Shar smiled, her cheeks pink. "You smell."

Feeling happier than he had in months, Everis paused to take in the homey kitchen scene. He gazed at the picture he wanted. A wife and kids in a comfortable home. If he played his cards right, he might just have the exact picture he saw. "I'll be back. Hope those cookies are done." He took the stairs two at a time, choosing to use the bath in Shar's room rather than the guest one downstairs. He didn't think it would be easy for Shar to climb stairs with her stitches.

He set the shower spray to hot, and stripped. Within minutes, he'd washed the smell of throw-up from his body and rinsed it out of his shirt. The ladies would have to ogle his chest until the shirt was washed and dried. He grinned, remembering the look on Shar's face. He didn't think she'd mind.

He tossed the shirt in the wash, poured in the detergent and headed back to the kitchen.

Shar sat at the kitchen table, Robby on her shoulder, Brian next to her with a cookie in one hand. Across from them sat Mira with a hint of a smile on her face.

"Smells good," he said, snagging one. "Chocolate chip. My favorite."

"I might be a messy baker," Mira said, "but I can bake."

"I'll remember that." He tossed her a wink. His cell rang. "Hey, Mayfield."

"Not sure the sheriff told you, but I'm investigating a possible sighting of Smith. She was long gone, but it was definitely her and the baby she took. I've asked the surrounding shop owners to call immediately if she shows up again. Anything else?"

Everis locked gazes with Shar. "No, that's about it. I'll do some more questioning in the morning. Maybe we'll catch this woman the old-school way. By pounding the pavement." He hung up and explained the call to Shar.

"I could get my homies to look for her," Mira offered. "They can find anyone if they're in the area."

Shar grinned. "That's a great idea, Mira."

"Good. I'll go there now."

"No, ma'am. We'll go tomorrow. You're staying here until I know you have a safe place to stay."

Which, if Everis thought correctly, would most likely be a long time. Shar had a tender heart for kids, even sullen ones. Mira wouldn't be leaving. "I'll take you tomorrow, I promise."

"Candy has the day off." Shar put a hand on Goliath's head. "Between her and Big Boy here, the babies will be safe."

"That dog scares me." Mira tossed him a cookie. "So, I'll win his affection through food."

They all laughed.

Everis's phone rang again. "Wow, I'm a popular man today." The screen said private number. "Agent Hayes."

"This is your final warning, agent. I want my son."

Chapter Nineteen

After tracing Smith's phone last night, and discovering it was an unregistered phone tossed in a trash bin downtown, Shar and Everis now sat in her jeep with Mira and stared at the Springs apartments. "Are you sure your friends hang out here?"

Mira leaned over the front seat. "Yep, this is the slums of Highland Springs. Well, this and the trailer park. Are we getting out or not?"

Shar was starting to believe they needed to hire a full-time officer to patrol the apartment complex. "We're going." She exited the jeep and paused to catch her breath after a sharp pain reminded her to take things easy.

"I saw that," Everis said. "You should have stayed home."

"I'm the sheriff, and I won't hide behind a bullet hole."

"Y'all fight over it later. Let's go. If we wait too late, they'll all have gone on to do their...uh, business." Mira pushed open the gate and stalked off.

Shar sighed and headed after her. She glanced at Brian's mother's apartment, relieved not to see the woman hanging over the banister. The last thing Everis needed was a confrontation. They were there to find a way to catch the elusive Smith.

Curtains parted as they passed. Doors slammed. Curses were shouted. Shar slipped her sheriff mask into place and took note of everything happening around her. Finally, Mira stopped at the far back corner of the complex and knocked on a door.

A young black man answered the door, cursed and tried to slam it shut. Mira stuck her foot in the way. "They're here to get help, JoJo, not arrest anyone. I swear."

"You'd better not be setting me up." He opened the door.

Shar counted eight young men and two women sleeping on furniture and on the floor. She mentally added talking to the leasing manager to her to-do list. The apartment was too small for that number of people.

She focused her attention on JoJo while Everis took up a silent position next to the door. "I'm sure you're aware of the woman who is stealing babies and selling them. Am I correct?"

"Yeah, so?" He crossed his arms.

"We have reason to believe she's in this area. Mira assured us that you could find anyone."

He flicked a glimpse at Mira, then nodded. "Yeah. What's in it for me?"

"Knowing you did the right thing." She held his gaze without blinking. "Time is of the essence. Will you help us?"

"What do y'all think?" He turned to his roommates.

"I say yes," a girl said. "What if the baby belonged to one of us? We'd want help, right?"

"Fine, sheriff. We'll hunt down this woman."

Shar smiled. "Thank you." She handed him a business card with her cell number on it, then scribbled Everis's. "Please call either me or the agent with any news, no matter how small."

"Is it true you're adopting Mira's baby?" JoJo asked.

"Yes, why?"

"Just seems strange is all."

She tilted her head. "Why? I want a child, and he's beautiful. Thank you for your willingness to help." She motioned her head for Mira to follow, then left the apartment.

Outside, she turned to the girl. "Will they do it?"

"Yeah. JoJo might be gangsta, but he always keeps his word." She lowered her voice. "There are a couple of apartments on the other side of this lot that are closed for renovations."

Shar glanced at Everis. "Worth a look?"

"Anything is worth a look." He put a hand on Mira's shoulder. "Go wait in the jeep and lock the doors."

"Nobody here is going to hurt me." She glowered.

"No, but Rachel Smith might."

Her eyes widened. With a nod, she darted away.

"Do you really think she'd come after Mira?" Shar's heart skipped a beat.

"If Smith were to take Mira, she'd have you and Robby, not to mention me, right where she wants us. Firmly in her grip."

Shar turned and headed across the dirt lot to a strip

of six rooms. "These used to be part of an old motel." It would take a lot of work to convert them into something worth living in.

An old man came around the corner and stopped, surprise registering on his face. "What's up, sheriff?"

"May we look in these rooms?"

"Sure." He removed a ring of keys from his belt. "The owner purchased them about a month ago, but we haven't started renovations. We've got to put in kitchenettes and the supplies ain't come in yet." He handed her the keys. "I'll be over there cleaning up garbage, so we can pour a new parking lot. Yell when you're done."

"Thanks." The chances of Smith actually living in a place like this were slim, but desperate people did desperate things. "After this, we need to head to the drugstore where she was seen last." She opened the first door.

Nothing but concrete floor and drywall full of holes. The next two were the same, except one had been stripped down to dirt. The fifth room had a stained mattress, a marijuana pipe, and used paper dishes. Someone had been here, but not Smith. She'd guarantee it.

After dry swallowing a couple of ibuprofen, she followed Everis back to the jeep. Mira was in a hot embrace with JoJo. "Ah, I think we've found Robby's baby daddy," Shar said, her stomach giving a lurch. That would explain the young man's interest in her adopting the baby.

She cleared her throat. "We're leaving, Mira. You may come or go. Your choice." She speared JoJo a sharp glance. "If she stays for a while, you do not leave her side for anything. Got it?"

"Yes, ma'am. Ain't nobody gonna hurt my girl."

"Make sure." Shar climbed into the driver's seat. "Call when you want to be picked up."

"Thanks, Sheriff." Mira flashed a rare grin.

Shar exhaled slowly through her nose. "Staying with me is your choice, Mira. You aren't a prisoner." Once Everis climbed in, she backed from the spot and headed toward Main Street.

* * *

Everis stood on the corner and stared down the street. How had only one person seen Smith? It wasn't exactly a bustling center of commerce. He shook his head, followed Shar into the drugstore, and stepped back into time.

A counter, complete with a soda fountain, stretched along one wall. A few round tables filled the front of the store. The actual drugstore didn't start until halfway in. "I'm going to share a malt with you one of these days," he said.

Shar bumped him with her shoulder. "I'll accept."

They headed side by side to the pharmacy counter where a young woman worked the register. She wore a lab coat, but there was no way she was old enough to be a pharmacist. "Where's the person who should be at this register?"

She jerked her head up. "My grandfather is in the back. I'm just keeping an eye on things."

Shar stepped up to the counter. "Take off the coat and step on this side of the counter, please. Unless you're older than you look, you aren't legal to be back there."

"Okay." She slung the coat over a chair and darted

159

through the door separating the pharmacy from the rest of the store.

"Don't go anywhere," Everis said. He reached over and tapped the bell on the counter.

Within minutes, an older man hurried toward them, drying his hands on a towel. "Good morning, Sheriff. Sir." He grinned. "Amy."

"Sir, your granddaughter was behind the counter working the register." Everis fixed the man with a hard stare.

His smile faded. "We've talked about this, Amy. What did you take today?"

"Just a couple of Percocets."

He narrowed his eyes. "How did you get the combination?"

She hung her head. "I watched you. That woman pays good money for them."

"What woman?" Shar drew the girl's attention to her.

"The one taking the babies. She pays me fifty bucks a pill." The girl's eyes darted to the pharmacist.

His face darkened. "I've had enough of her stealing. Sheriff, I'd like to press charges."

"Grandpa!"

"I'm sorry, Amy." He turned his back to her.

More importantly, they needed to know where Amy was going to meet Smith. Everis held out his hand. Once the girl dropped five bills into his hand, he gave them to the pharmacist. "Where were you going to meet Rachel Smith?"

"Nowhere. I leave the pills near a fallen tree by the lake and she leaves the money."

"Mayfield is on his way to take Amy into custody,"

Shar said. "Looks like we're making a trip to the lake."

Tears poured down the girl's face. "She only makes the exchange at night."

"Are you the one who called in that she'd been spotted?"

"I did." The pharmacist said. "I had no idea of what was going on with that woman and Amy."

Knowing about the girl's involvement explained a lot, but not everything. "How did Smith get out of here without anyone else seeing her?"

"I let her out the backdoor in the supply room." Amy covered her face. "I only wanted to save money to buy a car."

"There are other ways." Shar took her by the arm and accompanied her to the front door where Mayfield had pulled up to the curb.

"Thank you for your help." Everis gave the older man a nod and moved outside.

He stood on the sidewalk and again glanced up and down the street. Smith had a car, but she wouldn't be far away. No, she needed easy access to infant supplies, not to mention electricity and a way to warm bottles.

"What are you thinking?" Shar slammed the door on Mayfield's car.

"We've alerted every business and private citizen the best we can, and Smith still manages to evade us. She needs food and gas. Those are necessities. Where is she getting her supplies?"

"If we knew that, we'd have her behind bars. Let's question the store owners across the tracks. There's a convenience store I've busted a few times for selling liquor to minors." Shar strode back to the jeep, Everis at her side.

Ten minutes later, they stood in front of a very nervous old man with more wrinkles than a map that had been wadded up and run over with a truck. "Mr. Ryan," Shar said. "When did you start carrying baby formula?"

He avoided her gaze. "A year or so ago."

"Right about the time Rachel Smith moved to Highland Springs?" Everis asked.

"Coincidence."

Shar removed handcuffs from her belt. "I'm arresting you for obstruction of justice. You knowingly sold supplies to a fugitive of the law. Turn around and put your hands behind your back." Her eyes glittered like sapphires, a sure sign she was very angry. "We will close you down for this, sir."

From the rigidness of her back, Everis could tell it took all her willpower not to forcefully remove the man. Everis grabbed his other arm and put him into the back of the jeep. He glanced over the vehicle roof at Shar. "Eventually, there won't be any unscrupulous people left in Highland Springs to help this woman."

"That won't happen fast enough for me."

* * *

"Stupid girl." Rachel glared as the teen laughed and flirted with a young man. She'd be pregnant again soon. Would the sheriff keep every baby the girl pushed out?

The young man was staring at Rachel over his girlfriend's shoulder. He narrowed his eyes. Did he recognize her? She wore a wig and sunglasses. Surely a gangster couldn't care enough about an old white woman to retain any details.

Regardless, the way he watched her sent shivers down her spine. She needed to lay low until she could put the next part of your plan into place.

One of the deputies drove by, not sparing Rachel a second glance. Sitting in the backseat was the stupid girl who supplied Rachel with her meds. She cursed and slapped the steering wheel. Things were growing too hot. No one would step forward to be her supplier now for any amount of money.

Already pain rose up her back and beat at her skull. Doctors had told her the ache was all in her mind. She knew better. Something rancid ate away at her. The only thing keeping it at bay were the meds.

She glanced in the rearview mirror tilted at just the right angle to give her a clear view of Darcy. How was she going to take proper care of her daughter if the pain took over? Too much pain made mama a violent woman.

Chapter Twenty

Shar put Robby to bed and, after taking a pain med that would help her relax for four hours, eased herself into her chair. The long day had left her aching. She rested her head against the chair back and closed her eyes.

"Sheriff."

Mira's shaky voice had Shar reaching for her weapon on the side table. It wasn't there.

Rachel Smith, hat pulled low over her forehead, held an infant girl in one arm, and held a gun in the other hand pointed at Mira's head. "First things first, Sheriff Camenetti. I know you must have some pain meds. I need them." A fire burned in her eyes. "Don't try anything funny, or I'll shoot this worthless teenage mother."

Shar narrowed her eyes and got to her feet. The bottle of pain meds was on the kitchen counter. No need to head down the hall and alert the crazed woman to the fact that…Robby chose that time to cry. Shar closed her eyes and held her breath.

"Go get the baby, sheriff." Rachel motioned with the gun. "We'll follow to make sure you don't try to call your agent friend. I'm serious about shooting this girl."

"I'm sorry, sheriff." Tears streamed down Mira's cheeks. "She grabbed me as I was coming in the back door."

"It's not your fault, Mira." Shar entered what used to be the guest room, but now functioned as a nursery, and lifted Robby from the crib. "Don't worry, sweetie. We'll get you changed and fed in no time." And find a way to get rid of the woman holding Shar's gun.

"Pack the baby some diapers and formula," Smith said. "We aren't staying here, and Darcy doesn't have enough to share."

Shar shot the woman a look. "I'll take them all, then." She laid Robby on the bed and tossed the needed items into a duffel bag. "The pills are in the kitchen." She lifted the baby and led the way out of the room.

"Great." Smith smiled without humor. "Let's go."

Shar glanced at the clock on the way, then glared at Mira. "Three a.m.?"

She shrugged. "I fell asleep."

Smith scoffed. "Enough chitchat."

Snatching the bottle of pain meds, Shar dropped them into the bag and shoved open the back door. If only Smith had arrived three hours later. Everis might have shown up in time when he picked Shar up for work.

Smith herded them to Shar's jeep. "You're driving, Sheriff. I'll be sitting in the back with those you care about. Don't drive crazy. Darcy will be in the baby seat. Your son won't."

Fighting back the urge to head-butt the woman and take her chances on getting shot, Shar slid into the driver's seat and waited for the order to drive. She should never have succumbed to the pain. Falling into a deep sleep had not only allowed a crazy person to take her weapon, but to kidnap her family.

Wait. Candy. Where was she? Shar glanced at the house. Safely asleep, or had she stayed the night with Pinson? Had their relationship progressed to that level?

The window blinds parted at the front window, then fell back into place. Her sister was home.

"Mira, go get the sheriff's sister. I'll have the gun pointed at you the entire time. You'd best run. I'm sure people will be coming." Smith kicked open the jeep door. "Go!"

Mira raced for the house. One minute later, a glowering Candy came to the jeep and stumbled into the front passenger seat. Smith now had everyone Shar cared about, except for Everis.

"Drive north, Sheriff." Rachel slapped the back of her seat. "I'll let you know where to turn." The woman popped a couple of pills without water. "Just a car full of girls out for a jaunt."

"Hardly." Shar drove from the driveway and cut a sharp glance at Darcy. "Tell me you called for help," she whispered.

Candy nodded. "Pinson is contacting the others."

Shar blinked, wondering why Everis hadn't been the first one called.

"I see the question in your eyes. Because he has a child to find a sitter for."

"My son." Smith kicked the back of the seat. "He has my son, and you two ladies are going to help me get him back."

Not a chance. Shar would make sure, somehow, that

167

the fewest people possible would suffer from Smith finally showing herself.

"Turn right."

Smith guided them to an overgrown meadow. Shar recognized the trapdoor. They were at the exit to the Victorian house.

"We're staying here for a few hours," Smith said. "Then, we'll put the rest of my plan into action."

She herded them to the trapdoor and into the tunnel. "I know it's dark, but there's nowhere to go but forward." A light flared to life on the brim of her hat. "Continue until you reach the room behind the fireplace. That's where we'll stop for a few hours."

When Shar held back in the hopes of trapping Smith between her and Darcy, she got the barrel of the gun rammed into her stitches. The pain drove her to her knees. She felt a stitch pop, and wetness spread across her ribcage.

"Get up, and don't be a hero." Smith tapped the gun on her head.

"I'm going to make you pay for that."

Smith laughed. "I know you're going to try." She slid a bar across the opening to the fireplace.

* * *

"Say that again." Everis sat up.

"Smith has Shar and the rest of her household," Pinson said. "Candy was able to call me, but now she isn't answering."

Everis scrambled to get out of bed, the sheet tangling around his legs. He stumbled, then hopped, finally kicking off the blanket. "I need a babysitter, man."

Pinson chuckled. "Call Amber. She'll watch your

boy."

"Good idea. Meet me at the office. Call Mayfield." Everis dialed Amber who said she could be there in fifteen minutes, then rushed to get dressed. Where would they start their search? Smith could have taken them anywhere.

The moment Amber arrived, Everis sped to the office. "Find out if Smith owns other property," he ordered, striding into the conference room. "She has to have taken them somewhere. Try tracking cell phones. Put out an APB on Sheriff Camenetti's car."

"Working on it," Mayfield said.

Pinson handed Everis a cup of coffee. "The sheriff is clever. She'll get out of this."

"Not if it puts the children in danger." Everis took a sip of the bitter coffee and burned his tongue. He felt as useless as a newborn baby.

The office phone rang. Mayfield snatched it from its cradle, listened, then hung up. "A group of kids up to no good on the highway spotted the sheriff's car heading north. Said they heard the alert over a police scanner."

"Let's go, Pinson. Mayfield, man the office and keep us updated." He dashed to his rental car, Pinson on his heels.

The man groaned as he lowered himself into the passenger seat. "I'm not up to running marathons yet."

"I won't wait for you." Everis slammed the car into gear, tires squealing as they left the parking lot.

"I don't expect you to. Smith has my gal, too."

Everis nodded. Fifteen minutes out of town, they stopped next to a pickup truck full of underage kids. "Boys."

"Are you going to arrest us?"

"Not this time. Although, if I find out you drove home drunk as skunks, I'll make sure you're locked up for a while. Tell me about seeing the sheriff's jeep."

"Yeah, it sped by here going way over the speed limit. But we could see that the car was full of people. They kept going north."

Everis couldn't drive aimlessly. They needed a plan. A place to search. He turned the car toward the large Victorian, hoping, praying he wouldn't have to go into the tunnel.

Yellow crime-scene tape waved at them as they drove up. A large padlock still bolted the front door shut. They were here, so they might as well investigate until Mayfield called them with another lead.

He unlocked the padlock on the door and entered, clicking on the flashlight he'd pulled from his pocket. He shined it across the dust-covered floor. No footprints, other than rodents, marred the floor. Just as he'd thought. Smith hadn't returned to the place it all began.

"It's a pity how this old beauty is falling into ruin," Pinson said. "I wonder if it's for sale. I could probably fix it up."

"You can look into that later. We have people to save." Everis turned to leave when he heard a faint cry. He held out an arm to stop Pinson. "Did you hear that?"

"Hear what?"

The cry came again. "That." Everis ran his hands over the fireplace. "They're behind here. Shar and I discovered the secret passage. It's where the Smiths held their captives." Why wouldn't the door open? "It won't budge."

"Maybe if we both try." Pinson put his good shoulder against the mantle and pushed. It slid, but fell back into place. "It's blocked from the other side."

"The exit. Let's go." Everis pulled his weapon and tore across the back lawn.

* * *

Shar pressed her arm against the wound in her side. The baby girl had started to cry, and Smith bounced her against her shoulder and made shushing sounds.

Scrambling noises came from the fireplace.

Smith cursed. "Up and out. Right now. Let's go. Why can't a woman catch a break?" She waved the gun toward Candy. "Get your sister up and moving or I shoot her. Girl, grab the baby you birthed and let's go. If that agent shows up before I have my son, I'll shoot every single one of you."

Shar believed her. Desperation shone from the woman's eyes. She'd killed before and would do it again if it suited her purpose. Using the wall for support, Shar stood and headed back down the tunnel.

"We'll have to escalate things a bit," Smith said once they were in the car. "Head to the day care."

Shar shifted in her seat. "Why?"

"Because I said so." Smith held the gun to the back of Candy's head.

Mira started to cry.

"Shut up. I have need of you or you'd be dead, girl." Smith popped another pill from the bottle. "What I don't understand is why people don't get what I'm about. I'm here to save the children. Can't y'all see that? I save them from unfit mothers and give them to those who can take proper care of them."

"You sell them." Shar said, peering into the

rearview mirror. "Don't pretend there is anything at all good about your selfish motives. You're a rich woman. You got rich by breaking the law and have ruined families because of it."

"Think what you want." Smith smiled down at the baby girl. "I'm doing a good thing."

Smith ordered Shar to park a couple of blocks away from the day care. Keeping to the shadows, they made their way behind the building.

"Get us inside, sheriff."

"How do you propose I do that?" Shar frowned. "I don't have a key."

"Pick it."

She started to protest, when Mira stepped up. "I can do it." She pulled a pin from her pocket and set to work. Ten minutes later, they stepped into the back room of the day care and settled down to wait. For what? Only Smith knew.

Everis had stopped taking Brian there the moment he realized Smith wanted him back.

Smith paced the small supply room, muttering under her breath. Instead of the pain meds calming her, they seemed to agitate her.

Shar reached over and grasped her sister's hand. It was quite possible none of them would make it out alive.

Chapter Twenty-One

Here we go! Rachel rubbed her sweaty palm down the thigh of her pants, then switched the gun to her other hand and repeated the process. The first worker had arrived.

As each person entered, Rachel smiled and showed the gun. They cooperated right away after that. Then, the lovely children started arriving. By eight a.m., she was ready to put her plan into action.

"Lock the front door, please, and everyone gather in this main room. Quickly now." She stepped into the open. "Then, someone hand me the phone."

While the children and teachers crowded into the room, Rachel took care to stay well behind them in case the agent got smart and hired a sniper. She smiled at a curly-haired little girl. "I could fetch quite a pretty penny for you, darling. But I can tell your mommy loves you very much." She dialed the number to the sheriff's office.

"This is Rachel Smith. I have control over the Highland Springs Little Angels Day Care. Please have Agent Hayes call me." She hung up before the deputy could stop stuttering.

Everis stood at the entrance to the dark tunnel and tried not to throw up. He stared into the darkness. A cold sweat broke out on his forehead and upper lip.

His phone rang, yanking him from his thoughts. "Hayes."

"Uh, yeah. Smith took over the day care and wants you to call her."

"Ok." Everis hung up and sprinted for his car.

"Really?" Pinson shook his head. "I just got here."

"We have to get to the day care." As they ran, Everis called Smith. When she answered, he said, "You asked for me?"

"Very good. I like people who do what they're told."

"What do you want?"

"You know what I want. I have a day care full of children, workers, the sheriff and her sister, the teenage mother, and babies. So, here's the deal. You bring me my son, or I start eliminating those in here with me. You have one hour." Click.

He couldn't give her Brian. By doing so, he might as well pull the trigger on Shar and the others himself. The only good thing about Smith's demands was that she considered Brian hers and would take care of him. She wouldn't really kill the other children, would she?

He sped to the day care and parked across the street. Staying behind the cover of the rental car, he dialed the day care again. "Let me speak to the sheriff."

"Where's my son?"

"I have someone getting him."

"Liar." A gunshot rang out. "That was a warning shot, agent." Click.

Everis punched the hood of the car. "Have Amber bring me my son." He closed his eyes and leaned his forehead against the car. He'd have to trust a killer at her word. Something that went against every ounce of sense he possessed.

Twenty minutes later, Amber led Brian by the hand. Tears shimmered in her eyes. "Are you sure?"

"I'll get him back safe." He had to believe that he would. "Take him into the drugstore and wait. Turning him over is the last resort."

Pinson leaned against the car. "I've called Little Rock. We need to stall her for at least two hours. Less if they send a chopper. SWAT from Hot Springs will be here faster."

The faces of children became plastered against the front window as they stood in a straight line and stared out. Behind them, Mira, eyes wide in her ebony face, crossed her arms and hunched her shoulders. A woman—a teacher, Everis presumed—stood next to her, then another and another, ending at Candy. "She built a wall," he said.

"Smart woman," Pinson said. "She had to have known we would call in the guns."

There was absolutely no way to get to her. "I'm going around back. I have my phone." Staying low, Everis sprinted around the building.

There was no sign of Shar's jeep. They must have arrived under the cover of darkness after parking somewhere else. He tried the back door. Locked, which was not a surprise. He stepped back and studied the brick siding. No way up.

He turned and moved to the opposite side. An iron ladder scaled the back of the building. If he had something to stand on, he could be on the roof within minutes. A ladder meant roof access. Thank God for small towns and old buildings.

He hurried back to Pinson. "Once SWAT arrives, I'm going up. Do not bring Brian to me or that woman unless I say."

"Code word."

He frowned. "What?"

"Give me a code word so I know you aren't being forced, and that you really mean it." Pinson grinned.

"Okay." Everis raised his eyebrows. "*Pinson is a poor excuse for a deputy* means move in. *You're a crazy old bat* means take the shot. *Take care of my son* means she's going to kill me and I have no way of making it out alive. *You win* means bring me Brian."

"I'll never remember all that."

"You'd better because I'm going to be inside that building within the hour."

Shar grabbed a towel from a shelf and stuffed it in her shirt to help with the little bit of bleeding. Then, with one hand against the wall for support until she caught her breath against the pain, she moved to the front room.

Standing taller than most of those in the room, she could see Pinson and Everis across the street. The deputy didn't look pleased with what Everis was saying. Shar could only hope he wasn't going to do something foolish and get himself killed.

She moved to where Robby lay on a pallet. The little girl, not Darcy as Smith insisted on calling her, lay next to him. At least, Smith didn't kill children. That soothed Shar's heart some to know Robby wouldn't be harmed, nor would he know the drama playing out around him.

"Sit down, Sheriff." Smith, gun close at hand, sat behind the front desk. She leaned back and propped her feet on the desktop. "Your man still has a little over an hour to meet my demands. You might just be rescued before you bleed to death."

Shar glared in her directionand remained standing. She couldn't see if she sat down, and she needed to know what was happening outside. Shar wasn't sure what she could possibly do with a roomful of children captives, but if an opportunity presented itself to be of help to those outside and in, she would take it.

A SWAT van pulled up across the street, and armored men poured from the back of it. One of them scaled a ladder and positioned himself with a sniper rifle on the roof.

"So, it begins." Smith let her feet fall to the floor and picked up the gun. She rolled her head on her shoulders, then approached the day care director, an older woman around the age of fifty. "I choose you." She pushed the woman toward the door. "I'm going to open the door, and you're going to walk out. Easy, right?"

"Don't do this, Rachel." Shar took a step forward.

The director started to cry.

"Now look what you've done, Sheriff." Smith shook her head. "You've taken away her hope." She opened the door just enough for a person to squeeze through. She gave the woman a shove. "Go."

As soon as the woman reached the strcct, Smith took aim and fired. The woman dropped to the pavement.

The phone on the desk rang. Smith pivoted and grinned. "Worked like a charm."

Shar glanced across the street to see Everis with his phone to his ear.

"This is Rachel Smith," she said as if she were answering for a customer. "I had to, agent. Don't you see? You needed to know how serious I really am. Fine. I suppose." She handed the phone to Shar.

"Are you okay?" Everis asked.

"I'm fine."

"We're coming up with a plan to get all of you out of there."

"That sounds good. We'll be here."

Smith wiggled her fingers. "That's enough. He wanted to know you still breathed. He does."

Shar handed her the phone.

Smith hung up and resumed her seat at the desk. "I sure hope he can tell time. I can't abide crying in adults, and those women haven't stopped since I came in."

"You're cold." Shar leaned her back against the wall next to Robby. The children milled around, but enough stayed in front of the window to make getting a good shot difficult.

Mira visibly trembled.

Candy took her hand.

"I'm doing what has to be done." Smith opened desk drawers. "Yes." She held up a candy bar. "I'm famished." She ripped off the paper with her teeth and took a bite.

"I'm sure the children are, too."

"It is their snack time," one of the workers said. "May I get a box of graham crackers from the supply closet?"

"No, Mira can get it. She needs to be useful."

Mira scurried to the closet.

Shar was torn between hoping the girl would dash out the back door or stay and not anger Smith. Mira returned, but cast a glance at Shar that clearly said she'd done something. She handed each child a graham cracker, then resumed her spot at the window.

Ducking her head to hide a smile, Shar steadied her breathing. She should know that a teen from the streets wouldn't go down easy.

"They'll need drinks and potty breaks," the worker said.

"Mira can do that, too." Smith yawned loudly,starting to look bored. "I almost hope your agent man tries something."

"He won't hand over his son."

"Of course, he will. It's only a matter of time. The child is already in the drugstore waiting for his alleged father to give the okay."

"How do you know this?" Was Everis bugged?

"I saw that slutty receptionist of yours escort him down the sidewalk." She grinned. "I'm not psychic."

Shar slipped her mask into place. She couldn't reveal a single thought to this woman, or she would use it against her. When Robby and the infant girl started to fuss, she concentrated her efforts on making them happy. As long as Smith stayed behind the desk, no one was dying.

When she'd finished, she stood and inched closer to the window. Her gaze met Everis's. he flicked his gaze toward the roof.

Ice water poured through Shar's veins. He was coming in. Everis had to know there was no way out for him once he did. He wouldn't be able to take Smith down unless he entered the front of the day care center.

Candy must have noticed the same thing. Her eyes widened, and she stiffened.

Mira stepped back, sidling closer to Shar. "I took the chain off the back door," she whispered. "Next time, I'll throw the bolt."

"No. You can't risk yourself like that."

"No talking. Sheriff, resume position near the babies." Smith stood. The woman was fortunate to be short enough as to not easily be seen through the window.

Shar wanted to give her a big push that rammed her against the glass and gave those across the street a clean shot. Instead, she watched as the woman played the coward and hid behind frightened children.

By now, a crowd had gathered outside. Reporters and frantic parents. Some voices were loud, women cried. They were all living the stuff of any parent's nightmare. Shar could do nothing but stand and let her strength bleed from her.

Chapter Twenty-Two

Rachel counted the heads in the room. There didn't seem to be as many children between her and the window as there once was. Mira had been taking them in groups to the bathroom, and…. "Where are the other children?" She stood and pointed the gun at Mira.

The sheriff glanced up, her skin unnaturally pale, and stepped between the gun and the teen. "They're all here."

"No, they aren't. I'm not blind." Oh, why hadn't she counted at the beginning? Things were getting a little fuzzy. How many pills had she taken? "One, two, three…" what came next? "Seven." They had to all be there. Where could they have gone? "No more bathroom. They can all wear diapers." She glanced at the clock. Time was up.

"So, who is going to walk out that door now?"

The phone rang, and she grabbed it. "Time's up."

"I know, but we've run into a complication. Brian is here. You can see him out the window."

She glanced out and saw her son standing on the sidewalk. "His name is Devin."

"Fine. He's scared and has had an accident. I need to get him changed and calmed down. Give me another thirty seconds. Please. You can see he's here. Just thirty feet from you." The agent kept one hand on Devin's head. Her son looked quite distraught.

"Okay. It's lunch time. Change him, feed him, and send him to me. No more stalling." She slammed the phone down. "This is taking too long."

She studied the other children. She could take one of them. There was another dark-haired boy, but he wasn't Devin. She slumped in her chair. The boy across the street wasn't hers either. Neither was the baby she called Darcy. She glared at the sheriff. It was all her fault. She was the one causing Rachel to doublethink things.

Clutching the gun, she started to pace.

* * *

Everis took Brian to Amber in the drugstore, then ran around back to the child care. The back door hung open a few inches. He grinned. Someone was helping him. Just as he started to go inside, he spotted a little girl peering from behind the dumpster. Then another, then a boy. "What in the world?"

He ran over and counted ten children five and under. Getting into the building would have to wait. He spoke into his radio. "I've got some of the children. No idea how they got outside, but someone needs to come get them before I can progress."

"On my way," Pinson said. In less than five minutes, he drove a van to the back of the building and loaded the children inside. "Good luck." He gave Everis a nod and drove away.

He was going to need it. Pulling one weapon from

its holster and leaving another under his shirt in the waistband of his pants, he edged the back door open. The building was unnaturally quiet. Usually, a day care was filled with the cries and laughter of children.

Today, the place reeked with fear. Cries were quickly hushed.

Sliding along the wall, he peeked into the front of the building. Smith paced from one end to the other waving her gun and muttering. Occasionally, she stopped and glared at Shar. Everis's heart skipped a beat.

Shar still stood, but she slumped against the wall next to Robby and another baby. Blood seeped through the tan of her uniform shirt. Pain etched lines in her face.

Everis needed to get her out of there. When she glanced his way, he motioned his head toward the back door.

She shook her head. Her gaze flicked to Robby. Of course, he should have known she wouldn't leave her son on any condition. He'd do the same under the circumstances.

Through the window he could see Pinson unloading the children. Idiot. Smith would—

"What in the hell?" Smith stopped and glared out the window. "How did they—" she whirled to Mira. "I ought to shoot you next." She dashed toward the hall, skidding to a stop when she spotted Everis. Her gun hand swung to Shar. "Put down your weapon, agent."

Everis set the gun on the desktop. He put his hands up.

"Over there. On the wall opposite the sheriff." Smith's eyes shone with an unnatural light. Her steps had become sluggish, her speaking slurred. "I really need to take a break." Keeping a shaky hand holding a gun in Shar's direction, she sat behind the desk and shook a pill from a bottle.

Maybe all he had to do was wait long enough and she'd overdose on whatever it was she was popping.

"Now, the way I see it, Mr. Agent Man, is that I'm going to have to shoot you for not complying with my demands. I don't like shooting law enforcement. Do you know what they do to cop killers in prison?"

"I've heard stories."

"That is why I'm hesitant and haven't killed the sheriff. I know she's been cooking up a plan in that pretty head of hers. I can tell." She gave a sly grin. "She wants to kill me, I think." She sighed. "I honestly don't think any of us will make it out of here alive."

"Why do you say that?"

"Because I came prepared. If things get too hairy, I'll set this place on fire. We'll all go up in flames."

The woman was crazier than Everis had thought. Insane people were dangerous and unpredictable. He caught sight of the sniper on the roof across the street. If he could get Smith to stand in his line of vision…

"You're a silly man, agent," Smith said, training the gun on him. "I'm getting tired of holding this."

"Put it down and save us all a lot of grief."

"Yeah, you'd like that. Really, all I wanted was children. My entire life I wanted a son and daughter, then my girl was taken from me. This is nothing more than an exaggerated repeat of that horrible day."

"It doesn't have to be," Shar said. "We can all walk away from this."

"I'll go to prison."

"Yes, you will," Everis added, "but you can find others to help. Women who are missing their own children."

"Women not fit to have children." She stood. "I'm the Child Saver. I take the poor, the unwashed, the unwatched, and give them to those who will give them a better life. Just as I had planned to do with my own children. Life sometimes throws you a nasty curve, doesn't it?"

* * *

Shar's side ached, but the bleeding had stopped. She was nowhere near as weak as she pretended to be. All she needed was an opportunity to present itself.

Everis motioned toward the window.

Shar nodded. Somehow, they'd get Smith over there. "Candy, could you come here, please?"

Stepping back, Candy came to Shar's side. "You okay?" she whispered. "You look like death."

"So do you."

"I'm scared pitless." She cut a sideways glance at a narrowed-eyed Smith. "She's just waiting for a chance to shoot you."

"I need you to cause a distraction of some kind to draw her near the window. Something that would cause me to respond and her to follow."

"A meltdown?"

Shar smiled. "Something like that."

"What are you two whispering about?" Smith approached them. "Get away from each other."

"I'm getting my sister a drink of water. The little ones are thirsty, too."

"Nope. The last time I let someone out of my sight, they let kids escape." She whacked Mira in the back of the head with the butt of her gun. The girl crumbled the floor. Before Shar could react, the gun was pointed at Candy. "Back to the window."

"Please don't shoot me." Tears poured down Candy's cheeks. She should have been an actress. "I'll do whatever you say. Please." She wailed and ran to the window. Doubling her fists, she pounded on the glass. "Help me, help me."

"Shut up." Confusion clouded Smith's drugged eyes. When Candy continued her cries, Smith took a step forward. "Stop it."

Candy fell to the floor, hiding behind several children. "I can't. Please don't kill me."

"Get up. You're a coward." Another step toward the window.

Shar moved away from the wall. Good girl, Candy. She knew Smith wouldn't shoot the children.

"Tell your sister to get off the floor." Smith glanced over her shoulder.

Shar froze. "Candy, calm down."

"Listen to the sheriff." Smith turned back to the window.

Shar launched herself at the woman's back, driving her forward and into the glass. Almost immediately, Everis was there to help.

"Look up at that building, Smith." Shar pressed the woman's face against the window. "See that sniper? All I have to do is take a step away from you and he will put a bullet in your head. Do you understand?"

Smith nodded. "You are going to be very sorry, sheriff."

"Candy, you and the teachers get the children out. Now."

One of the women threw open the front door and started ushering children across the street. Candy grabbed Robby and the other baby. "Shar?"

"Go, Candy."

"Um, there's a bomb in the baby's diaper bag."

"Get out." Shar's heart dropped to her feet. "The children come first. Save them."

Candy spun around, a baby in each arm, and ran.

"Where's the ignition?" Shar pressed Smith's face harder until her teeth ground against the window.

"It's on a timer. I knew the agent wouldn't hand over the boy." Smith laughed. "It goes off at high noon."

Shar glanced at the clock, then at Everis. "Two minutes."

He radioed across the street for them to all take cover. Then, leaving Smith to fend for herself, he grabbed Shar's hand and ran.

The force of the explosion knocked them to the asphalt. When Shar was able to breathe again, she sat up and stared at the building. A fire-engulfed Rachel Smith stood in the destruction, laughing, arms raised over her head.

"That's going to cause some nightmares," Everis said, getting to his knees. "Are you alright?"

"I am now." She got to her feet and searched for Candy. "Where is everyone?"

"Hopefully crowded inside the SWAT van. It's the only place they had time to get to." Everis opened the door.

Team members, children, and adults, packed in like sardines, blinked against the light. "It's over, folks."

Sirens wailed in the distance. Shar took a pain-filled

step toward the onlookers. They'd been rained with glass, but other than what looked like minor cuts, seemed unharmed. She held up her hands and whistled to get their attention. "Ladies and gentlemen. I know you are anxious to retrieve your children. Let us get organized, then we'll let you do so. Please be patient. It's been a rough morning."

Pressing her hand against her again bleeding side, Shar shuffled to where the children and teachers gathered on the sidewalk. She smiled into the face of her son. "I am so glad you are too young to be traumatized by this." The other children wouldn't be so lucky.

Three hours later, with a fresh bandage on her gunshot, Shar handed the last child over to his parents. Exhaustion coated her limbs. Her head pounded. She wanted nothing more than to go home and sleep with Robby by her side.

Everis must have felt the same way. He held Brian in his arms and rested his chin on his son's head. He held out his free hand.

Shar gladly stepped into his one-armed embrace. "We really need to find a better way to spend time together."

He chuckled. "I agree, but I don't see us sitting in front of the television watching game shows. Not when life is this exciting on the streets of Highland Springs."

"I need a vacation."

"How about the four of us head to South Carolina? I know a great place on the beach." He lowered his head and kissed her.

Epilogue

Shar propped her bare feet on the deck railing of their rental and stared at the sun setting over the Gulf of Mexico. She grasped a glass of red wine in her hand.

Everis stepped onto the deck and placed a soft kiss in the curve of her neck. "Beautiful."

"It is." She lifted her glass toward the water.

"I was talking about you." He lowered himself into the chair beside her. "I've never seen you more relaxed."

She tilted her head. "You've never seen me not working."

"True. We've chased killers from the moment we met." He took a swig of his beer, his Adam's apple bobbing. His dark hair fell forward over his eyes, not slicked back in its usual fashion. He wore low-slung swim trunks and nothing else. He was easily the sexiest thing she'd ever seen.

"Your sister called," he said. "Mira is staying home more."

"That's good." After the terror in the day care, the teen hadn't been herself. Shar had set up several

189

therapist appointments and been appointed guardian. She'd gone from a woman alone to a single mother of a teen and a newborn in the matter of a week.

Everis held out his hand.

She placed hers in his. "Just say it."

"Say what?"

"There's been something you've wanted to say for two days. You've also spent more time on the phone than a man on vacation should." This was it. He was going to tell her he was leaving again. Each time he came to Highland Springs, she knew it was only for a while. He had another life in another place.

"With all the recent crime in Highland Springs, you've been awarded a third deputy." His eyes twinkled.

She frowned. "Who is it?"

"Me." He grinned.

"What?"

"I'm staying and raising my son in Highland Springs. The job of agent would take me away from home too much."

She had to look like an owl the way she stared. "Can you stand working for me?"

"Can you stand having me around?"

She squeezed his hand. "You know I'd like nothing better."

"Are you willing to see where a more permanent relationship between us might go?" He lifted her hand and placed a kiss in the palm. "Will you be my girl?"

She laughed. "We're much too old for that kind of talk, Everis Hayes."

Her phone rang. She answered after noticing it was Mayfeld. "This had better be good."

"I thought you and Hayes might like to know that most of the children have been returned to their biological mothers."

She leaned her head against the back of the chair and closed her eyes. "How horrible for the adoptive parents."

"Some of the biological parents agreed to legally sign their children over to the only parents the children know. Some adoptive parents are going to court. It's a mess, but one that is slowly being put to rights."

The pain Rachel Smith had caused to so many people left an ache in Shar's heart she wasn't sure would go away. She'd gained a son and a daughter from the ordeal, but so many weren't as lucky. She ducked her head and wiped away a tear. "Thanks for letting me know." She hung up and told Everis about the phone call.

His pleased expression faded. "It feels wrong to be so happy when others have had their lives torn apart."

"I agree."

Robby cried from inside the bungalow, spurring Shar to her feet. "Life goes on, and we have the promise of a good one." She smiled down at him. "I'm glad you're going to be working for me. I'll try to be a kind boss."

He grinned. "You couldn't be anything but." He pulled her down for a kiss, one that lingered a moment and pushed away the bad thoughts.

Then, he released her to tend to her son.

She stopped at the door and let her gaze land on him as he stared out at the water. Yes, she was very glad indeed that he was staying.

The End

Stay tuned for book three in the Highland Springs series.

ABOUT THE AUTHOR

www.cynthiahickey.com

Cynthia Hickey is a multi-published and best-selling author of cozy mysteries and romantic suspense. She has taught writing at many conferences and small writing retreats. She and her husband run the publishing press, Winged Publications. They live in Arizona and Arkansas, becoming snowbirds with three dogs. They have ten grandchildren who keep them busy and tell everyone they know that "Nana is a writer."